About Nina Harrington

Nina Harrington grew up in rural Northumberland, England, and decided at the age of eleven that she was going to be a librarian—because then she could read *all* of the books in the public library whenever she wanted! Since then she has been a shop assistant, community pharmacist, technical writer, university lecturer, volcano walker and industrial scientist, before taking a career break to realise her dream of being a fiction writer. When she is not creating stories which make her readers smile, her hobbies are cooking, eating, enjoying good wine—and talking, for which she has had specialist training.

My Greek Island Fling

Nina Harrington

First published in Great Britain 2012
by Mills & Boon, an imprint of Harlequin (UK) Limited,
Eton House, 18-24 Paradise Road, Richmond, Surrey TW9 1SR

© Nina Harrington 2012

ISBN: 978 0 263 22743 7

wable
ainable
the

Also by Nina Harrington

When Chocolate is Not Enough
The Boy is Back in Town
Her Moment in the Spotlight
The Last Summer of Being Single
Tipping the Waitress with Diamonds
Hired: Sassy Assistant
Always the Bridesmaid

Did you know these are also available as eBooks?
Visit www.millsandboon.co.uk

PROLOGUE

'MUM—I'm here,' Lexi Collazo Sloane whispered as her mother breezed into her room, instantly bringing a splash of purple, bravado and energy to the calm cream and gold colour scheme in the exclusive London hospital.

'I am *so* sorry I'm late, darling,' her mother gushed, shaking the rain from her coat and then planting a firm kiss on Lexi's cheek. 'But our director suddenly decided to bring the rehearsal of the ballroom scene forward.' She shook her head and laughed out loud. 'Pirate swords and silk skirts. If those dresses survive intact it will be a miracle. And don't talk to me about the shoes and wigs!'

'You can do it, Mum.' Lexi chuckled, folding her pyjamas into her overnight bag. 'You're the best wardrobe mistress in the theatre business. No worries. The dress rehearsal tomorrow will be a triumph.'

'Alexis Sloane, you are the most outrageous fibber. But, thanks. Now. Down to more important things.' She took a breath, then gently put a hand on Lexi's shoulder and looked into her eyes. 'How did it go this morning? And don't spare me. What did the specialist say? Am I going to be a grandmother one of these fine days?'

Lexi sat back down on the bed and her heart wanted to weep. Time to get this over and done with.

'Well, there's some good news, and some less-than-good news. Apparently medical science has advanced a little over the past eighteen years, but I don't want you to get your hopes up.' She reached out and drew her mother to sit next to her on the bed. 'There is a small chance that I might be able to have children, but...' she caught her breath as her mother gasped '...it would be a long, tough process—and there's no guarantee that the treatment would be a success in the end. According to the specialist, I'd only be setting myself up for disappointment.'

She braved a half smile and squeezed her mother's hand. 'Sorry, Mum. It looks like you might have to wait a lot longer before I can give you those grandchildren after all.'

Her mother exhaled loudly before hugging her. 'Now, don't you worry about that for one more minute. We've talked about this before. There are lots of children out there looking for a loving home, and Adam is happy to adopt. You *will* have your own family one day—I just know it. Okay?'

'I know, but you had such high hopes that it would be good news.'

'As far as I am concerned it *is* good news. In fact, I think we should splash out on a nice restaurant this evening, don't you? Your dad will insist,' she added, waggling her eyebrows. 'It seems the photography business is paying well these days.'

Lexi touched her arm and swallowed down the huge lump of anxiety and apprehension that had made an already miserable day even more stressful. 'Is he here yet, Mum? I've been nodding off all afternoon and now I'm terrified that I might have missed him.'

But her mother looked into her face with a huge grin. 'Yes,' she replied, clasping hold of both of Lexi's hands. 'Yes, he *is* here. I left your dad back in the car park. And he is so different. He really does want to make up for lost time. Why else would he pay for this lovely private hospital at the first mention that you needed treatment? He knew how scared you must be after the last time. Everything's going to be just fine. You wait and see.'

Lexi's heart started to race. 'What if he doesn't even recognise me? I mean, I was only ten the last time he saw me. That was eighteen years ago. He might not even know who I am.'

Her mother patted her cheek, shaking her head. 'Now, don't be so silly. Of course he'll recognise you. He must have albums filled with all of the photos I've sent him over the years. Besides, you're so lovely he'll spot you in an instant.'

She pressed her cheek against Lexi's as she wrapped her in a warm hug. 'Your dad has already told me how very proud he is of everything you've achieved in your life. And you can tell him all about your brilliant writing over dinner tonight.'

Then she patted her hair, snatched up her bag and headed into the bathroom. 'Which means I need to get ready. Back in a moment.'

Lexi smiled and shrugged her shoulders. As if her mother could ever be anything other than gorgeous! She'd aways been so irrepressible, no matter what life had thrown at them. And all she'd ever wanted was a large family around her whom she could shower with love.

Lexi wiped away a stray tear from her cheek. It broke her heart that she wouldn't be able to give her mother grandchildren and make her happy. Just broke her heart.

Mark Belmont stabbed at the elevator buttons, willing them to respond, then cursed under his breath and took off towards the stairs.

The logical part of his brain knew that it had only been

seconds since he'd thanked his mother's friend for keeping vigil in that terrible hospital room until he arrived. The steady weeping hadn't helped him to keep calm or controlled, but he was on his own now, and it was his turn to make some sense of the last few hours.

The urgent call from the hospital. The terrible flight from Mumbai, which had felt never-ending, then the taxi ride from the airport, which had seemed to hit every red light in London on the way in.

The truth was still hard to take in. His mother, his beautiful, talented and self-confident mother, had taken herself to a London plastic surgeon without telling her family. According to her actress friend she had made some feeble joke about not alerting the media to the fact that Crystal Leighton was having a tummy tuck. And she was right. The press were only too ready to track down any dirty secrets about the famously wholesome English movie star. But to him? That was his mother the tabloids were stalking.

Mark took the stairs two at a time as his sense of failure threatened to overwhelm him.

He couldn't believe it. They'd been together for the whole of the Christmas and New Year holiday and she'd seemed more excited and positive than she'd been in years. Her autobiography was coming together, her charity work was showing results and his clever sister had provided her with a second grandchild.

Why? Why had she done this without telling anyone? Why had she come here alone to have an operation that had gone so horribly wrong? She'd known the risks, and she'd always laughed off any suggestion of plastic surgery in the past. And yet she'd gone ahead and done it anyway.

His steps slowed and he sniffed and took a long breath, steadying himself before going back into that hospital room where his lovely, precious mother was lying comatose, hooked up to monitors which beeped out every second just how much damage the embolism had done.

A stroke. Doing what they could. Specialists called in. Still no clear prognosis.

Mark pulled open the door. At least she'd had the good sense to choose a discreet hospital, well-known for protecting its patients from prying eyes. There would be no paparazzi taking pictures of his bruised and battered mother for the world to ogle at.

No. He would have to endure that image on his own.

Lexi had just turned back to her packing when a young nurse popped her head around the door. 'More visitors, Miss Sloane.' She smiled. 'Your dad and your cousin have just arrived to take you home. They'll be right with you.' And with a quick wave she was gone.

'Thank you,' Lexi replied in the direction of the door, and swallowed down a deep feeling of uncertainty and nervousness. Why did her father want to see her now, after all these long years? She pushed herself off the bed and slowly walked towards the door.

Then Lexi paused and frowned. Her cousin? She didn't have a cousin—as far as she knew. Perhaps that was another one of the surprises her dad had lined up for her? She'd promised her mother that she would give him a chance today, and that was what she was going to do, no matter how painful it might be.

Taking a deep breath, she straightened her back and strolled out into the corridor to greet the father who had abandoned her and her mother just when they'd needed him most. If he expected her to leap into his arms then he was sorely mistaken, but she could be polite and thank him for her mother's sake, at least.

If only her heart would stop thumping so hard that she

could hardly think. She'd loved him so much when she was little—her wonderful father had been the centre of her world.

She braced herself and looked around. But all was calm, restful and quiet. Of course it would take a few moments for him to get through the elaborate security checks at the main desk—designed to protect the rich and famous—and then take the elevator to the first floor.

She was just about to turn back when she caught a movement out of the corner of her eye through the half-open door of one of the patient's rooms identical to the one she had just left, but tucked away at the end of the long corridor.

And then she saw him.

Unmistakable. Unforgettable. Her father. Mario Collazo. Slim and handsome, greying around the temples, but still gorgeous. He was crouched down just inside the room, under the window, and he had a small but powerful digital camera in his hand.

Something was horribly wrong here. Without thinking, she crept towards the door to get a better look.

In an instant she took in the scene. A woman lay on the hospital bed, her long dark hair spread out against the bleached white sheets which matched the colour of her face. Her eyes were closed and she was connected to tubes and monitors all around the bed.

The horrific truth of what she was looking at struck Lexi hard and left her reeling with shock, so that she had to lean against the wall to stay upright.

The nurses wouldn't have been able to see her father from the main reception area, where a younger man she had never seen before was showing them some paperwork, diverting their attention away from what was happening in this exclusive clinic under their very noses.

When she found the strength to speak her words came out in a horrified shudder. 'Oh, no. No, Dad. Please, no.'

And he heard her. In an instant he whirled around from where he was crouching and glared at her in disbelief. Just for a moment she saw a flash of shock, regret and contrition drift across his face, before his mouth twisted into a silent grin.

And her blood ran cold.

Mario Collazo had made a name for himself as a celebrity photographer. It wasn't hard to work out what he was doing with a camera inside the hospital room of some celebrity that he had stalked here.

If that was true... If that was true then her dad hadn't come to see *her* at all. He had lied to her warm-hearted mother and tricked his way into the hospital. None of the security officers would have stopped him if he was the relative of a patient.

Ice formed in the pit of her stomach as the hard reality of what she had just seen hit home. Her dad never had any intention of visiting her. The only reason he was here was to invade this poor sick woman's privacy. Lexi had no idea who she was, or why she was in this hospital, but that was irrelevant. She deserved to be left alone, no matter who she was.

Lexi felt bitter tears burning in the corners of her eyes. She had to get away. Escape. Collect her mother and get out of this place as fast as her legs could take her.

But in an instant that option was wiped away.

She had waited too long.

Because striding towards her was a tall, dark-haired man in a superbly tailored dark grey business suit. Not a doctor. This man was power and authority all wrapped up inside the handsome package of a broad-shouldered, slim-hipped man of about thirty. His head was low, his steps

powerful and strident to match the dark, twisted brow.
And he was heading straight for the room where her father was hiding.

He didn't even notice she was there, and she could only
watch in horror as he flung open the door to the woman's
room.

Then everything seemed to happen at once.

'What the hell are you doing in here?' he demanded, his
voice furious with disbelief as he stormed into the room,
pushed aside the visitor's chair and grabbed her father by
the shoulder of his jacket.

Her breath froze inside her lungs, and Lexi pressed her
back farther against the wall.

'Who are you, and what do you want?' His voice was
shrill and full of menace, but loud enough to alert the re-
ceptionist at the desk to look up and lift the telephone.
'And how did you get a camera in here? I'll take that, you
parasite.'

The camera came flying out of the door and crashed
against the wall next to Lexi with such force that it smashed
the lens. To Lexi's horror she saw the young man at reception reach into his pocket and pull out a digital camera and start to take photographs of what was happening
inside the room from the safety of the corridor. Suddenly
the stillness of the hushed hospital was filled with shout-
ing, yelling, crashing furniture and medical equipment,
flower vases smashing to the floor, nurses running and
other patients coming out of their rooms to see what the
noise was all about.

Shock and fear overwhelmed her. Her legs simply refused to move.

She was frozen. Immobile. Because, as if it was a horrible train wreck, she simply could not take her eyes away
from that hospital room.

The door had swung half closed, but she could see her father struggling with the man in the suit. They were fighting, pushing and shoving each other against the glass window of the room. And her heart broke for the poor woman who was lying so still on the bed, oblivious to the fight that had erupted around her.

The door swung open and her father staggered backwards into the corridor, his left arm raised to protect himself. Lexi covered her mouth with both hands as the handsome stranger stretched back his right arm and punched her father in the face, knocking him sprawling onto the floor just in front of her feet.

The stranger lunged again, pulling her father off the ground by his jacket and starting to shake him so vigorously that Lexi felt sick. She screamed out loud. 'Stop it— please! That's my dad!'

Her father was hurled back to the ground with a thud. She dropped to the floor on her knees and put her hand on her father's heaving chest as he pushed himself up on one elbow and rubbed his jaw. Only then did she look up into the face of the attacker. And what she saw there made Lexi recoil in horror and shock.

The handsome face was twisted into a mask of rage and anger so distorted that it was barely recognisable.

'Your *dad?* So that's how it is. He used his own daughter as an accomplice. Nice.'

He stepped back, shaking his head and trying to straighten his jacket as security guards swarmed around him and nurses ran into the patient's room.

'Congratulations,' he added, 'you got what you came for.'

The penetrating gaze emanating from eyes of the darkest blue like a stormy sea bored deep into her own, as though they were trying to penetrate her skull. 'I hope you're satisfied,' he added, twisting his lips into a snarl of disgust and contempt before looking away, as if he couldn't bear the sight of her and her father for a second longer.

'I didn't know!' she called. 'I didn't know anything about this. Please believe me.'

He almost turned, but instead shrugged his shoulders and returned to the bedroom, shutting the door behind him and leaving her kneeling on the cold hospital floor, nauseous with shock, fear and wretched humiliation.

CHAPTER ONE

Five Months Later

GOATS!

Lexi Sloane pushed her designer sandal hard onto the brake pedal as a pair of long-eared brown and white nanny goats tottered out in front of the car as she drove around a bend, and bleated at her in disgust.

'Hey, give me a chance, girls. I'm new around here,' Lexi sang out into the silent countryside, snorting inelegantly as the goats totally ignored her and sauntered off into the long grass under the olive trees on the other side of the road.

'Which girls? Lexi? I thought you were working.' Her mother laughed into her earpiece in such a clear voice that it was hard to imagine that she was calling from the basement of an historic London theatre hundreds of miles away. 'Don't tell me. You've changed your mind and taken off with your pals on holiday to Spain after all.'

'Oh, please—don't remind me! Nope. The agency made me an offer I couldn't refuse and I am definitely on Paxos,' Lexi replied into the headset, stretching her head forward like a turtle to scan the sunlit road for more stray wildlife. 'You know how it goes. I am the official go-to girl when it comes to ghostwriting biographies. And it's always at the last minute. I will say one thing—' she grinned '—I stepped off the hydrofoil from Corfu an hour ago and those goats are the first local inhabitants I've met since I left the main road. Oh—and did I mention it is *seriously* hot?'

'A Greek Island in June... I am *so* jealous.' Her mother sighed. 'It's such a pity you have to work, but we'll make up for it when you get back. That reminds me. I was talking to a charming young actor just this morning who would love to meet you, and I sort of invited him to my engagement party. I'm sure you'd like him.'

'Oh, no. Mum, I adore you, and I know you mean well, but no more actors. Not after the disaster with Adam. In fact, please don't set me up with any more boyfriends at all. I'll be fine,' Lexi insisted, trying desperately to keep the anxiety out of her voice and change the subject. 'You have far more important things to sort out without worrying about finding me a boyfriend. Have you found a venue for this famous party yet? I'm expecting something remarkable.'

'Oh, don't talk to me about that. Patrick seems to acquire more relatives by the day. I thought that four daughters and three grandchildren were more than enough, but he wants the whole tribe there. He's so terribly old-fashioned about these things. Do you know, he won't even sleep with me until his grandmother's ring is on my finger?'

'Mum!'

'I know, but what's a girl to do? He's gorgeous, and I'm crazy about him. Anyhow, must go—I'm being dragged out to look at gothic chapels. Don't worry—I'll tell you all about it when you get back.'

'Gothic? You wouldn't dare. Anyway, I look terrible in black,' Lexi replied, peering through the windscreen and slowing the car at the entrance to the first driveway she'd seen so far. 'Ah—wait. I think I've just arrived at my client's house. Finally! Wish me luck?'

'I will if you need it, but you don't. Now, call me the minute you get back to London. I want to know everything about this mystery client you're working with. And I mean *everything.* Don't worry about me. You just try and enjoy yourself. *Ciao,* gorgeous.'

And with that her mother hung up, leaving Lexi alone on the silent country lane.

She glanced up at the letters carved into a stone name-plate, then double-checked the address she'd noted down over the phone while waiting for her luggage to come off the carousel at Corfu airport, some five hours earlier.

Yup. This was it. Villa Ares. Wasn't Ares the Greek god of war? Curious name for a house, but she was here and in one piece—which was quite a miracle.

Checking quickly for more goats or other animal residents, Lexi shifted the hire car into gear and drove slowly up a rough gravel driveway which curved around a long, white two-storey house before coming to a shuddering halt.

She lifted off her telephone headset and sat still for a few minutes to take in the stunning villa. She inhaled a long breath of hot, dry air through the open window, fragrant with the scent of orange blossom from the trees at the end of the drive. The only sound was birdsong from the olive groves and the gentle ripple of water from the swimming pool.

No sign of life. And certainly no sign of the mystery celebrity who was supposed to have sent a minion to meet her at the hydrofoil terminal.

'Welcome to Paxos,' she whispered with a chuckle, and stepped out of the car into the heat and the crunch of rough stone beneath her feet.

The words had no sooner slipped from Lexi's lips than

the slim stiletto heel of her favourite Italian sandal scraped down a large smooth cobblestone, her ankle twisted over, and she stumbled against the hot metal of her tiny hire car.

Which left a neat trail of several weeks' worth of grime and bright green tree pollen all down the side of the Italian silk and linen jacket.

Oh, no! Grinding her teeth, she inspected the damage to her clothing and the scrape down her shoe and swore to herself with all of the fluency and extensive vocabulary of a girl raised in show business. The dark red leather had been completely scraped into a tight, crumpled ball down the heel of her shoe.

This project had better be a real emergency!

Even if it was so *totally* intriguing.

In the five years that she'd worked as a contract ghost writer this was the first time that she had been sent out on a top-secret assignment on her own—so secret that the publisher who'd signed the contract had insisted that all details about the identity of the mystery author must remain under wraps until the ghost writer arrived at the celebrity's private home. The talent agency was well-known for being extremely discreet, but this was taking it to the next level.

She didn't even know the name of her client! Or anything about the book she would be working on.

A tingle of excitement and anticipation whispered across Lexi's shoulders as she peered up at the imposing stone villa. She loved a mystery almost as much as she loved meeting new people and travelling to new places around the world.

And her mind had been racing ever since she'd taken the call in Hong Kong.

Who *was* this mysterious celebrity, and why the great secrecy?

Several pop stars just out of rehab came to mind, and

there was always the movie star who had just set up his own charity organisation to fight child trafficking—any publisher would be keen to have that story.

Only one thing was certain: this was going to be someone special.

Lexi brushed most of the pollen from the rough silk-tweed fabric of her jacket, then straightened her back and walked as tall as she could across the loose stone drive, the excitement of walking into the unknown making her buzz with anticipation.

A warm breeze caressed her neck and she dipped her sunglasses lower onto her nose, waggling her shoulders in delight.

This had to be the second-best job in the world. She was actually getting paid to meet interesting people in lovely parts of the world and learn about their lives. And the best thing of all? Not one of those celebrities knew that she used every second of the time she spent travelling and waiting around in cold studios to work on the stories she *really* wanted to write.

Her children's books.

A few more paying jobs like this one and she would finally be able to take some time out and write properly. Just the thought of that gave her the shivers. To make that dream happen she was prepared to put up with anyone.

Magic.

Swinging her red-leather tote—which had been colour-matched to her now-ruined sandals—she shrugged, lifted her chin and strode out lopsided and wincing as the sharp stones of the drive pressed into the thin soles of her shoes.

Hey-ho. They were only sandals. She had seen too much of the flip side of life to let a little thing like a damaged sandal annoy her. Meeting a client when she didn't even know their name was a drop in the ocean compared to the train wreck of her personal history.

It was time to find out whose life she was going to share for the next week, and why they wanted to keep their project such a secret. She could hardly wait.

Mark Belmont rolled over onto his back on the padded sun lounger and blinked several times, before yawning widely and stretching his arms high above his head. He hadn't intended to fall asleep, but the hot, sunny weather, combined with the latest bout of insomnia, had taken its toll.

He swung his legs over the lounger, sat upright, and ground the palms of his hands into his eyes for a few seconds to try and relieve the nagging headache—without success. The bright sunlight and the calm, beautiful garden seemed to be laughing at the turmoil roiling inside his head.

Coming to Paxos had seemed like a good idea. In the past the family villa had always been a serene, welcoming refuge for the family, away from the prying eyes of the media; a place where he could relax and be himself. But even this tranquil location didn't hold enough magic to conjure up the amount of calm he needed to see his work through.

After four days of working through his mother's biography his emotions were a riot of awe at her beauty and talent combined with sadness and regret for all the opportunities he had missed when she was alive. All the things he could have said or done which might have made a difference to how she'd felt and the decision she'd made. Perhaps even convinced her not to have surgery at all.

But it was a futile quest. Way too late and way too little.

Worse, he had always relished the solitude of the villa, but now it seemed to echo with the ghosts of happier days and he felt so very alone. Isolated. His sister Cassie had been right.

Five months wasn't long enough to put aside his grief. Nowhere near.

He sniffed, and was about to stand when a thin black cat appeared at his side and meowed loudly for lunch as she rubbed herself along the lounger.

'Okay, Emmy. Sorry I'm late.'

He shuffled across the patio towards the stone barbecue in his bare feet, watching out for sharp pebbles. Reaching into a tall metal bin, he pulled out a box of cat biscuits and quickly loaded up a plastic plate, narrowly avoiding the claws and teeth of the feral cat as it attacked the food. Within seconds her two white kittens appeared and cautiously approached the plate, their pink ears and tongue a total contrast to their mum. Dad Oscar must be out in the olive groves.

'It's okay, guys. It's all yours.' Mark chuckled as he filled the water bowl from the tap and set it down. *'Bon appétit.'*

He ran his hands through his hair and sighed out loud as he strolled back towards the villa. This was *not* getting the work done.

He had stolen ten days away from Belmont Investments to try and make some sense of the suitcase full of manuscript pages, press clippings, personal notes, appointment diaries and letters he had scooped up from his late mother's desk. So far he had failed miserably.

It certainly hadn't been *his* idea to finish his mother's biography. Far from it. He knew it would only bring more publicity knocking on his door. But his father was adamant. He was prepared to do press interviews and make his life public property if it helped put the ghosts to rest and celebrate her life in the way he wanted.

But of course that had been before the relapse.

And since when could Mark refuse his father anything? He'd put his own dreams and personal aspirations to one side for the family before, and would willingly do it again in a heartbeat.

But where to start? How to write the biography of the woman known worldwide as Crystal Leighton, beautiful international movie star, but known to him as the mother who'd taken him shopping for shoes and turned up at every school sports day?

The woman who had been willing to give up her movie career rather than allow her family to be subjected to the constant and repeated invasion of privacy that came with being a celebrity?

Mark paused under the shade of the awning outside the dining-room window and looked out over the gardens and swimming pool as a light breeze brought some relief from the unrelenting late-June heat.

He needed to find some new way of working through the mass of information that any celebrity, wife and mother accumulated in a lifetime and make some sense of it all.

And one thing was clear. He had to do it fast.

The publisher had wanted the manuscript on his desk in time for a major celebration of Crystal Leighton at a London film festival scheduled for the week before Easter. The deadline had been pushed back to April, and now he would be lucky to have anything before the end of August.

And every time the date slipped another unofficial biography appeared. Packed with the usual lies, speculation and innuendo about her private life and, of course, the horrific way it had been brought to an early end.

He had to do something—anything—to protect the reputation of his mother. He'd failed to protect her privacy when it mattered most, and he refused to fail her again. If anyone was going to create a biography it would be someone who cared about keeping her reputation and memory alive and revered.

No going back. No compromises. He would keep his promise and he was happy to do it—for her and for his family. And just maybe there was a slim chance that he would come to terms with his own crushing guilt at how much he had failed her. Maybe.

Mark turned back towards the house and frowned as he saw movement on the other side of the French doors separating the house from the patio.

Strange. His housekeeper was away and he wasn't expecting visitors. *Any* visitors. He had made sure of that. His office had strict instructions not to reveal the location of the villa or give out his private contact details to anyone.

Mark blinked several times and found his glasses on the side table.

A woman he had never seen before was strolling around inside his living room, picking things up and putting them down again as if she owned the place.

His things! Things he had not intended anyone else to see. Documents that were personal and very private.

He inhaled slowly and forced himself to stay calm. Anger and resentment boiled up from deep inside his body. He had to fight the urge to rush inside and throw this woman out onto the lane, sending her back whence she came.

The last thing he wanted was yet another journalist or so-called filmmaker looking for some dirt amongst his parents' personal letters.

This was the very reason he'd come to Paxos in the first place. To escape constant pressure from the world of journalists and the media. And now it seemed that the world had decided to invade his privacy. Without even having the decency to ring the doorbell and ask to be admitted.

This was unacceptable.

Mark rolled back his shoulders, his head thumping, his hands clenched and his attention totally focused on the back of the head of this woman who thought she had the right to inspect the contents of his living room.

The patio door was half-open, and Mark padded across the stone patio in his bare feet quietly, so that she wouldn't hear him against the jazz piano music tinkling out from his favourite CD which he had left playing on Repeat.

He unfurled one fist so that his hand rested lightly on the doorframe. But as he moved the glass backwards his body froze, his hand flat against the doorjamb.

There was something vaguely familiar about this chestnut-haired woman who was so oblivious to his presence, her head tilted slightly to one side as she browsed the family collection of popular novels and business books that had accumulated here over the years.

She reminded him of someone he had met before, but her name and the circumstamces of that meeting drew an annoying blank. Perhaps it was due to the very odd combination of clothing she was wearing. Nobody on this island deliberately chose to wear floral grey and pink patterned leggings beneath a fuchsia dress and an expensive jacket. And she had to be wearing four or five long, trailing scarves in contrasting patterns and colours, which in this heat was not only madness but clearly designed to impress rather than be functional.

She must have been quite entertaining for the other passengers on the ferry or the hydrofoil to the island from Corfu that morning.

One thing was certain.

This girl was not a tourist. She was a city girl, wearing

city clothes. And that meant she was here for one reason—and that reason was him. Probably some journalist who had asked him for an interview at some function or other and was under pressure from her editor to deliver. She might have come a long way to track him down, but that was her problem. Whoever she was, it was time to find out what she wanted and send her back to the city.

Then she picked up a silver-framed photograph, and his blood ran cold.

It was the only precious picture he had from the last Christmas they had celebrated together as a family. His mother's happy face smiled out from the photograph, complete with the snowman earrings and reindeer headset she was wearing in honour of Cassie's little boy. A snapshot of life at Belmont Manor as it used to be and never could be again.

And now it was in the hands of a stranger.

Max gave a short, low cough, both hands on his hips.

'Looking for anything in particular?' he asked.

The girl swung round, a look of absolute horror on her face. As she did so the photograph she was holding dropped from her fingers, and she only just caught it in time as it slid down the sofa towards the hard tiled floor.

As she looked at him through her oversized dark sunglasses, catching her breath unsteadily, a fluttering fragment of memory flashed through his mind and then wafted out again before he could grasp hold of it. Which annoyed him even more.

'I don't know who you are, or what you're doing here, but I'll give you one chance to explain before asking you to leave the same way you came in. Am I making myself clear?'

CHAPTER TWO

Lᴇxɪ thought her heart was going to explode.

It couldn't be. It just could *not* be him.

Exhaustion. That was the only explanation. Three weeks on the road, following a film director through a series of red-carpet events across Asia, had finally taken their toll.

She simply had to be hallucinating. But as he looked at her through narrowed eyes behind rimless designer spectacles Lexi's stomach began to turn over and over as the true horror of the situation hit home.

She was standing in front of Mark Belmont—son of Baron Charles Belmont and his stunningly beautiful wife, the late movie actress Crystal Leighton.

The same Mark Belmont who had punched her father in that hospital on the day his mother had died. And accused *her* of being his accomplice in the process. Completely unfairly.

When she was a little girl she'd had a recurring nightmare about being a pilgrim sent to fight the lions in some gladiatorial arena in Rome.

This was worse.

Her legs were shaking like jelly, and if her hand held on to her bag any tighter the strap would snap.

'What—what are you doing here?' she asked, begging and pleading with him in her mind to tell her that he was a temporary guest of the celebrity she had been paid to work with and that he would soon be leaving. Very soon. Because the other alternative was too horrible to imagine.

She'd thought that she had escaped her shameful connection to this man and his family.

Fate apparently had other ideas.

Fate in the form of Mark Belmont, who was looking at her with such disdain and contempt that she had to fight back the temptation to defend herself.

With a single shake of the head, he dismissed her question.

'I have every right to be here. Unlike yourself. So let's start again and I'll ask you the same question. Who are you and what are you doing in my house?'

His house? A deep well of understanding hit her hard and the bottom dropped out of Lexi's stomach.

If this was his house—was it possible that Mark Belmont was her celebrity?

It would make sense. Crystal Leighton's name had never left the gossip columns since her tragic death, and Lexi had heard a rumour that the Belmont family were writing a biography that would be front-page news. But surely that was *Baron* Belmont, not his business-guru son?

Lexi sighed out loud. She was jumping to conclusions—her imagination was running ahead of itself. This was a big house, with room for plenty of guests. It could easily be one of his colleagues or aristocratic friends who needed her help.

And then the impact of what he was asking got through to her muddled brain.

Mark had not recognised her. He had no clue that she was the girl he had met in the hospital corridor only a few months earlier.

They had only met for a few fleeting moments, and she

had certainly changed since then. They both had. And her sunglasses were a genius idea.

She inhaled a couple of breaths, but the air was too warm and thick to clear her head very much. It was as though his tall, powerful body had absorbed all the oxygen from the room.

A flicker of annoyance flashed across his full, sensuous mouth before he said, 'I don't take kindly to uninvited guests, so I suggest you answer my question before I ask you to leave.'

Uninvited guests? Oh, God, the situation was worse than she'd realised. He didn't seem to be expecting a visitor—any visitor. He had no idea that his publisher had sent a ghost writer out to the island! No wonder he thought that she was some pathetic burglar or a photojournalist.

Okay, so he had treated her unfairly in the worst of circumstances, but she was here to do a job. She glanced down, desperate to escape his laser-beam focus, and her eyes found the image of a happy family smiling back at her from behind the glass in the picture she had almost dropped.

It could have been a movie set, with a perfect cast of actors brought in for the day. Gorgeous film-star mother, handsome and tall aristocratic father, and two pretty children—with the cutest toddler on the planet waving at the camera. All grouped in front of a tall Christmas tree decorated in red and gold and a real fire burning bright in a huge marble fireplace.

What did Mark Belmont know about broken families and wrecked dreams?

Guilt about the pain her father had caused the Belmont family pinched her skin hard enough to make her flinch. But she ignored it. What her father had done had never been her fault, and she wasn't going to allow the past to ruin her work. She needed this job, and she'd be a fool to let her father snatch away the chance to make her dream come true.

Lexi opened her mouth as if to speak, closed it again, and then pinched her thumb and forefinger tightly against the bridge of her nose.

'Oh, no.' She shook her head slowly from side to side, eyes closed. 'The agency would *not* do this to me.'

'The agency?' Mark asked, his head tilted slightly to one side. 'Have you got the right villa? Island? Country?'

She chuckled, and when she spoke her voice was calmer, steadier.

'Let me guess. Something tells me that you may not have spoken, emailed or in some other way communicated with your publisher in the past forty-eight hours. Am I right?'

For the first time since she had arrived a concerned look flashed across his tanned and handsome face, but was instantly replaced by a confident glare.

'What do you mean? My publisher?'

Lexi dived into her huge bag, pulled out a flat black tablet computer, and swiped across the screen with her forefinger—being careful not to damage her new fingernails, which still carried the silver and purple glitter that had been the hit of the last show party in Hong Kong.

'Brightmore Press. Sound familiar?'

'Maybe,' he drawled. 'And why should that matter to me?'

Lexi's poor overworked brain spun at top speed.

He was alone in the villa. This was the correct address. And Mark *was* familiar with Brightmore Press. Lexi put those three factoids together and came up with the inevitable conclusion.

Mark Belmont was the mystery celebrity she had been assigned to work with.

And the bubble of excitement and enthusiastic energy that had been steadily inflating on the long journey from Hong Kong popped like an overstretched balloon.

Of all the rotten luck.

She needed the job so badly. Running a home in central London wasn't cheap, and this bonus would have made a big difference to how quickly she could start the renovations. All her plans for the future relied on having her own home office where she could write her children's books full-time. Walking away from this job would set her back months.

She stared at him wide-eyed for a few seconds, before sighing out loud.

'Oh, dear. I hate it when this happens. But it does explain why you didn't meet me at the harbour.'

Mark shifted his legs shoulder-width apart and crossed his arms. 'Meet you? No, I don't think so. Now, let me make myself quite clear. You have two minutes to explain before I escort you from my private home. And please don't think I won't. I've spent more time than I care to think about giving press conferences. My office has a catalogue of past interviews and press statements, covering every possible topic of conversation. I suggest that you try there—because I have absolutely no intention of giving you an interview, especially when you seem intent on damaging my property. Am I getting through to you?'

'Your property? Oh, I'm so sorry,' she murmured, scrabbling to pick up the picture and brushing off any dust from the silver frame. 'I did knock, but there was no answer, and the door was open. This is a lovely family photo and I couldn't resist peeking at it, so...' She gave a quick shrug of the shoulders and lifted her chin slightly. 'You should be more careful about security.'

'Really?' He nodded, his voice calculating and cool enough to add a chill to the air. 'Thank you so much for the advice, but you aren't in the city any more. We don't lock our doors around here. Of course if I'd *known* I was to have visitors I might have taken additional precautions. Which brings us to my earlier question. Who are you, and why are you here? I'm sure the two charming police officers who take care of this island would be delighted to meet you in a more formal setting. And, as you have probably realised, Gaios is only about three miles from here. And they are the proud owners of both a police car and a motorcycle. So I would suggest that you come up with a very convincing excuse very quickly.'

Police? Was he serious?

She looked warily into those startling blue eyes. Oh, yes, he was serious.

Her chest lifted a good few inches and she stared straight at him in alarm. Then she sucked in a breath and her words came tumbling out faster than she would have thought possible.

'Okay. Here goes. Sorry, but your peeps have *not* been keeping you up to date on a few rather crucial matters. Your Mr Brightmore called my talent agency, who called me with instructions to get myself to Paxos because one of their clients has a book to finish and they—' she gestured towards his chest with her flat hand '—are apparently a month past the final deadline for the book, and the publishers are becoming a little desperate. They need this manuscript by the end of August.'

She exhaled dramatically, her shoulders slumped, and

she slid the tablet back into her bag with a dramatic flour-
ish before looking up at him, eyebrows high, with a broad
grin.

'Right. Now that's out of the way I suppose I should introduce myself. Alexis Sloane. Otherwise known as Lexi.
Ghost writer *extraordinaire.* And I'm here to meet a client
who needs help with a book. I take it that would be you?'

'Well, of *course* I didn't tell you what the publisher had
organised, darling brother, because I knew exactly what
your reaction would be.'

Mark Belmont sat down hard on the end of the sun
lounger, then immediately stood up again and started pacing up and down the patio, the sun-warmed stone hot under
his bare feet. The temperature was a perfect match for
his mood: incendiary. His emotions boiled in a turmoil
of resistance, resolution and defiance touched with fury.
Cassandra Belmont had a lot to answer for.

'Cassie,' he hissed, 'I could strangle you. Seriously.
How could you do this to me? You *know* that this biography is too personal, too close to home, to ask anyone to
help. Why do you think I've come all the way to Paxos
to work on the book on my own? The last thing I need is
some random stranger asking questions and digging into
places I don't know I want to go myself. Communication is
a wonderful thing, you know. Perhaps you've heard of it?'

'Relax.'

His sister's voice echoed down the phone, and he imagined her curled up on the sofa in Belmont Manor while her
two small sons played havoc around her.

'Lucas Brightmore recommended the most discreet
agency in London. Their staff sign cast-iron confidentiality agreements and would never divulge anything you
tell them. I think it could work.'

'Cassie, you are a menace. I don't care how discreet this...*secretary* is. If I wanted a personal assistant I would have brought one. I have excellent staff working for me. Remember? And I would never, *ever* invite them here to the villa. I need privacy and space to get the work done. You know me.' His voice slowed and dropped lower in pitch. 'I have to get my head into the detail on my own before I can go public with anything. And I need peace and quiet to do that.'

'You're right. But this is not a business project you are evaluating. This is our mother's life story. It has to do her justice, and you're the only person in the family with the faintest bit of creativity. I know I couldn't do it in a million years. I don't have nearly enough patience. Especially when it comes to the difficult bits.'

Cassie took a breath and her voice softened.

'Look, Mark, this is hard for all of us. And it's incredibly brave of you to take over the project. But that makes it even more important to get the job done as quickly as you can. Then we can all get on with our lives and Dad will be happy.'

'Happy?' Mark repeated with a dismissive cough. 'You mean like he's happy about my plans to renovate those derelict cottages on the estate into holiday lets? Or the restructuring plans for the business that he's been blocking since Christmas?'

'Probably not,' Cassie answered. 'But you know as well as I do that it isn't about you or me. It has a lot more to do with the fact that he's ill for the first time in his life and he's just lost his wife in a surgical procedure she never even told him about. He doesn't know how to deal with that any more than the rest of us.'

Mark ran his tongue over his parched lips. 'How is he today?'

The delay before Cassie answered said more than the sadness inherent in her reply. 'About the same. This round of chemotherapy has really knocked him back.' Then her steely determination kicked back in, tinged with concern. 'You don't need to put yourself through this. Hand back the advance from the publisher and let some journo write Mum's biography. Come home and run your business and get on with your life. The past can take care of itself.'

'Some journo? No, Cassie. The press destroyed Mum's last chance of dignity, and I don't even want to *think* about what they'd do with a true-life *exposé* based on lies, innuendo and stupid gossip.' He shook his head and felt a shiver run down his spine despite the heat. 'We know that her friends have already been approached by two writers for hire looking for dirt. Can you see the headlines? Read All About It: The True Sordid Past of the Real Crystal Leighton Belmont.' He swallowed hard on a dry throat. 'It would kill him. And I *refuse* to let her down like that again.'

'Then finish the book our mother started. But do it fast. The agency said they were sending their best ghost writer, so be nice. I'm your sister, and I love you, but sometimes you can be a little intense. Oh. Have to go. Your nephews are awake and need feeding. Again. Take care.'

'You, too,' Mark replied, but she had already put the phone down.

He exhaled slowly and willed his heart rate to slow.

He had never been able to stay angry with Cassie. His sister had been the one constant in his father's life ever since their mother had died. She had her own husband, a toddler and a new baby to take care of, but she adored the manor house where they had grown up and was happy to make a home there. Her husband was a doctor at the local hospital whom Cassie had met when she'd taken their father for a check-up. Mark knew that he could totally rely on her to take care of their father for a few weeks while he took time out of the office.

She had even taken over the role of peacemaker on the rare occasion when he went back to Belmont Manor.

But she shouldn't have talked to the publisher without telling him about it.

Suddenly the decision to come to Paxos to finish the biography seemed ridiculous. He'd thought that being on his own would help, but instead he'd become more agitated and irritable by the day. He needed to do things. Make things happen. Take responsibility just like he'd always done. It infuriated him that he'd found it impossible to focus on the task he had set himself for more than a few minutes without having to get up and pace around, desperate for an opportunity to procrastinate.

Cassie was right. This biography was too close. Too personal.

His mother had always been a hopeless housekeeper, and organisation had never been one of her strong points. She'd liked the creative world, and enjoyed making sense of the jumble of random photographs, letters, newspaper clippings and memorabilia.

And he was just the same. An artist in many ways. His natural inclination was to push through the boundaries of possibility to see what lay beyond and shake things up. Little wonder that he was increasingly at loggerheads with his father's almost obsessive need to keep things in order. Compliant. Unchanging. Private and quiet.

Or at least that had been the case until six months ago. But now?

Now his father was on his second round of chemotherapy, his beloved mother had effectively died on a plastic surgeon's operating table, and his on-off girlfriend had

finally given up on him and met someone she actually
seemed to love and who loved her in return.

Mark felt as though the foundations on which he had
based his entire life had been ripped out from under him.

His fingers wrapped tightly around the back of the chair
until the knuckles turned white with the pressure.

No. He could handle this trauma. Just as he had abandoned his own life so that he could take his brother's place
in the family.

There was no point in getting angry about the past.

He had given his word. And he would see it happen on
his own, with the privacy and the space to work things
through. The last thing he needed right now was a stranger
entering his private space, and the sooner he persuaded
her that the publisher was wrong and she could head off
back to the city the better.

Think. He needed to think.

To stop herself shaking Lexi gripped her shoulder bag
with one hand and pressed the other against the back of the
leather sofa. She couldn't risk ruining her carefully con-
trived show of being completely unfazed as she looked at
Mark Belmont, pacing up and down the patio next to the
swimming pool, her cell phone pressed to his ear.

Only this was not the business-guru version of The
Honourable Mark Belmont that usually graced the covers
of international business magazines around the world. Oh,
no. She could have dealt with that stiff, formally dressed
office clone quite easily. *This* version was an entirely
different sort of man: much more of a challenge for any
woman.

The business suit was gone. Mark was wearing a pair
of loose white linen trousers and a short-sleeved pale blue
striped polo shirt that perfectly matched the colour of his

eyes. His toned muscular arms and bare feet were tanned as dark as the scowl he had greeted her with, and the top two buttons of his shirt were undone, revealing a bronzed, muscular chest.

His dark brown hair might have been expertly cut into tight curls, but he hadn't shaved, and his square jaw was covered in a light stubble much more holiday laid-back than designer businessman. But, Lord, it suited him perfectly.

She knew several fashion stylists who would have swooned just at the sight of him.

This was a completely different type of beast from the man who'd defended his mother so valiantly in the hospital. This was Mark Belmont in his natural setting. His territory. His home.

Oh, my.

She could lie and pretend that her burning red neck was simply due to the heat of a Greek island in late June and the fact that she was overdressed, but she knew better.

Her curse had struck yet again.

She was always like this around Adonis-handsome men. They were like gorgeous baubles on display in a shop window. She could ogle them all day but never dared to touch. Because they were always so far out of reach that she knew she would never be able to afford one. And even if she could afford one it would never match the disorganised chaos of her life.

This particular bauble had dark eyebrows which were heavy and full of concern. He looked tense. Annoyed and anxious.

It had seemed only right to ring the publisher for him. Just to clarify things.

Only judging by the expression on his face the news

that her assignment was not a practical joke after all had not gone down well.

Normally her clients were delighted that a fairy godmother had dropped into their world to help them out of a tricky situation.

Apparently Mark Belmont was not seeing his situation in quite the same way.

She had to persuade him to allow her to stay and help him with…with *what?* She still had no idea what type of book Mark Belmont was writing. Business management? A family history? Or…she swallowed…the obvious. A memoir of his mother.

Lexi looked up as Mark turned towards her from the door, lowering the phone, and searched his face for something—anything—that would help her make the decision.

And she found it. In his eyes of frosty blue.

The same eyes that had looked at her with such pain mixed with contempt on that terrible day in the hospital. When his heart had been breaking.

Decision made. If he could survive writing about his late mother then she would do her best to make the book the best it could be. Even without his help.

She could make this work. It would take a lot of effort, and she would have to be as stubborn as a stubborn thing in Stubbornland, but she could do it. She had stood her ground before, and she'd do it again.

Mark stood still for a moment, eyes closed, tapping the cell phone against the side of his head.

'If you're quite finished with my phone, Mr Belmont?' A sweet, charming voice echoed out from behind his back. 'It tends not to function very well after being used as a percussion instrument.'

Mark opened his eyes and stared at the offending cell phone as though he had never seen it before. He'd never used a purple phone in his life and he was extremely tempted to throw the offending article into the pool and leave it there. *With its owner. The hack writer.*

Fortunately for the phone, good manners kicked in and, holding it between his thumb and forefinger, he turned and extended his arm towards Lexi.

To her credit, she was not wearing a self-satisfied smirk but the same look of professional non-confrontational indifference he was used to seeing from city suits around the boardroom table where some of his riskier ideas were discussed.

Except for him this was not a job. It was very personal. And even the idea of sharing his deepest concerns and emotions about his parents made him bristle with resentment and refusal to comply.

He hadn't built a venture-capital company from the ruins of his father's business without taking risks, but they had been calculated risks, based on information he had personally checked and worked on until he'd known that the family's money would not be wasted on the investment.

This girl—this woman—in this ridiculous outfit had arrived at his home without his approval.

His sister might have confidence in the talent agency, but he knew nothing about the plan, and if there was one thing guaranteed to annoy him it was things being planned behind the scenes without his knowledge.

Cassie was perfectly aware of that fact, but she'd done it anyway. Her intentions might be excellent, but the reality was a little difficult to stomach.

A light tapping broke Mark out of his reverie, and he flashed a glance at the girl just in time to see her keying furiously into the cell phone, her sparkly purple-painted fingernails flashing in the sunlight. Although how she could see through those huge sunglasses was a mystery to him.

In the living room she had been more stunned than stunning, but in the bright white light reflected back from the patio her skin appeared pale and almost translucent, as though she hadn't seen sunlight for quite some time. The contrast between her English-rose complexion and the startlingly bright scarves wrapped around her neck was so great that it distracted him for a moment from the fact that she was talking.

'I'll be with you in a moment, Mr Belmont,' she said away from the phone. 'I'm just trying to find out the location of the nearest hotel on the island. Unless, of course, you can recommend one to me?'

She looked up and gave him a half smile—a pink-cheeked, polite kind of smile that still managed to brighten her whole face, drawing his full attention.

'I apologise for not booking accommodation before I arrived, but this assignment was rather last-minute. I'll need to stay somewhere close by, so I don't waste too much time travelling back and forth. Don't worry,' she added, 'I'll be out of your hair within the hour.'

'A hotel? That is quite out of the question,' he answered.

'Oh?' She raised her eyebrows and her fingers stilled. 'And why is that?'

Mark pushed his hands into his pockets to keep them from fastening around that pretty pale neck and squeezing hard.

'Well, for one thing there is indeed a small hotel in Gaios. But it is currently closed for over-running refurbishments. And secondly…' He paused before saying the words. 'Paxos is a very small island. People talk and ask questions. I hardly think it would be appropriate for you to stay in rented accommodation while you're working on a confidential project for the Belmont family. And I'm afraid that you certainly don't *look* like a package holiday tourist.'

To her credit, she didn't look down at her outfit to check if something was amiss. 'I don't? Excellent. Because I have no intention of looking like a tourist. I want to look like me. As for confidentiality…? I can assure you that I'm totally discreet. Anything you tell me will be in strict confidence. I've worked on many confidential projects, and none of my previous clients ever had any problems with my work. Now, is there anything else you'd like to know before I head to town?'

He lifted his chin and dropped his shoulders back, chest out, legs braced, creating the sort of profile his media consultants had recommended would be perfect to grace the covers of business magazines. Judging by the slight widening of her eyes, it was equally effective on the patio.

'Only this. You seem to be under the illusion that I've agreed to this arrangement. That is not the case. Any contract you might have is between my publisher and your agency. I certainly haven't signed anything. And I have a big problem with being railroaded. Which is exactly how I'm feeling right now. I dislike surprises, Miss Sloane.'

She lifted her chin, and instantly the firmness of the jawline on her heart-shaped face screamed out to him that this was a girl who rarely took no for an answer.

'It's unfortunate that you weren't expecting me,' she replied with a tight smile, 'but I can assure you that I have no plans to return home before this assignment is completed.'

She reached into the tiny pocket of her jacket, pulled out a small business card and presented it to him. 'I've just survived two long international flights, one hour on the hydrofoil from Corfu, and twenty minutes negotiating car hire with the charming Greek gentleman at the port to get here. I don't intend to leave until my boss instructs me to. So. May I suggest a compromise trial period? Let's say twenty-four hours? And if you don't find my services valuable, then I promise to jump into my hire car and get out of your life. One day. That's all I'm asking.'

'One day?' Mark echoed through gritted teeth.

'Absolutely.'

A smile warmed her lips, and for the first time since they'd met it was a real smile. The kind of smile that made the Cupid's-bow curve of her full lips crinkle girlishly at the edges and the pink in her cheeks flush with enjoyment. She was enjoying this. And she was clearly determined to make him do all the work.

'Very well. Twenty-four hours it is. In which case there is only one possible option,' he continued. 'You will be staying here at the villa with me until I decide whether I need your help or not, Miss Sloane.'

CHAPTER THREE

'You want me to stay here at the villa?' Lexi looked around the patio, then back towards the house. 'You did say you lived here alone, Mr Belmont? Is that correct? I'll take your silence as a yes. In that case, aren't you worried about what your wife or girlfriend will think about the arrangement? A single man living here alone suddenly has a young lady houseguest? There are bound to be questions.' Lexi glanced at him. 'Perhaps you have nieces?'

'I'm afraid not. Two nephews. Both under five. Go by the names of Charles and Freddie.'

'Shame.' She nodded and screwed up her face. 'How about cousins? Old schoolfriends? Casual acquaintances that just happen to pass by?'

'No subterfuge will be necessary, Miss Sloane. You can call yourself a business colleague or personal assistant for as long as you stay here. Take your pick.'

'Business colleague it is. Personal assistant smacks too much of a girl who organises your dry-cleaning, runs your office and buys presents for your lucky lady-friends—of which I'm sure there are many.'

Lexi leaned forward slightly towards Mark.

'I don't actually perform those particular duties, by the way. In case you're wondering. Ghostwriting. That's it. Okay? Splendid. Now, seeing as I'll be staying here, would you mind helping me with my suitcases? I do have quite a few.'

'What do you mean a few?'

Mark strolled over to the edge of the patio and stared at the tiny hire car. Lexi tottered past him and descended the two low steps that curved down to the driveway.

'You men have it easy.' She laughed, opening up the boot and heaving the two massive matching cases out onto the pebble driveway. 'A couple of suits and that's it. But I've just spent three weeks on the road with different events every evening.'

A cabin bag and a leather Gladstone bag followed.

'Clients expect a girl to wear different outfits for each film launch to keep the photographers happy,' she added, walking around to the passenger door and flinging it open. The top garment bag had slipped a little down the back of the driver's seat, so she tugged it free and folded it over one arm before grabbing hold of her travel bag with one hand and slinging the shoulder strap of her overnight case across the front of her jacket.

Lexi pushed the car door closed with one foot and looked around for Mark. He was standing open-mouthed, still watching her from the terrace as though he could hardly believe what he was looking at.

Lexi rolled her eyes, took a firmer hold of her bag and tottered across the pebbles of the car park onto the patio steps. 'Don't worry about me,' she said, 'I've left the heavy bags down by the car. Any time today will be good.'

'No problem,' Mark murmured under his breath. 'The porter will be right with you.'

He reached for his shoes, which he had stashed under the lounger. Unfortunately, as he bent over, Lexi tottered past his very fine rear end in her high-heeled sandals, and as he stood up his elbow jogged the overnight bag she was carrying.

At exactly the same moment the slippery silk fabric of her garment bag slipped down her arm. She snatched at it with the hand holding the travel bag, twisting her body round to stop it from falling to the ground.

And she took one step backwards.

The stiletto heel of her right sandal hit the smooth marble edge of the swimming pool, her right leg shot forward, she completely lost her balance and instinctively flung both arms out to compensate.

For one millisecond she was airborne. Arms twirling around in wide circles, both legs in the air, luggage thrown out to each side and the thin silk fabric of her overdress inflated up to her waist as a parachute.

She squeezed her eyes tight shut and prepared herself for a dunking in the swimming pool. But instead her feet lifted even higher off the ground as a long, strong arm grabbed her around the waist and another arm swept under her legs, taking her weight effortlessly.

Lexi flashed open her eyes, gave a high squeak of terror, and flung both her arms around Mark's neck by sheer instinct, pressing herself tight onto his shirt. Unfortunately she forgot that she was still clutching her travel bag for dear life, and succeeded in hitting Mark on the back of the head with it.

To his credit, he gave only a low, deep sigh instead of yelling like a schoolboy.

She opened her mouth to apologise, then closed it again. Her lungs seemed to have forgotten how to work and her breathing had become a series of short panting noises— which would have been perfect for a spaniel but which, from her lips, managed to sound both pathetic and wheezy at the same time.

She had *never* been picked up before.

And the last time she'd been this close to a handsome man had been on Valentine's night, when her ex-boyfriend had confessed he'd been sleeping with a girl she'd thought was her friend. So it would be fair to say that it hadn't ended well.

This, on the other hand, was turning out to be a much more positive experience.

Below his loose blue shirt Mark was muscular, warm and solid against her body, and in the position he was holding her their faces were only inches apart. His eyes locked onto hers, and suddenly it made perfect sense just to lie there in his arms while he took her weight.

Up close, she could see that his eyes were not a perfectly clear blue, as his mother's had been, but were flecked with slivers of darker blue and grey, so that under the shade of the terrace they looked like a cloudy summer sky.

His wiry dark brown hair was curled at the base of his neck with the heat of the afternoon, and she inhaled an intoxicating aroma of some fragrant shampoo or shower gel, freshly laundered linen shirt and something much deeper and muskier.

She had no clue what it was, but that extra something had the power to make her heart beat faster than was probably safe. So fast that it was all too easy to recall that she was here to work. Not to cuddle the client or to partially strangle him with her arms after trying to knock him out.

'I should have warned you about the pool. Are you okay now?' he asked, his voice low with concern.

She swallowed, and gave a smile and a short nod. Instantly the arm around her waist slackened and her brief adventure came to a halt as he slowly lowered her back down and her sandals made contact with solid ceramic tile.

Strange how her arms seemed reluctant to lose contact

with Mark's shirt and practically slid the full length of his chest—before the sensible part of her brain took over and reminded her that her agency contract included some rather strict rules about fraternising with the clients.

Lexi tugged down on the hem of her dress and pretended to be straightening her clothing before daring to form actual words.

'No problem. I prefer not to go swimming fully clothed, so thanks for saving me from a dunking. And sorry about the bag.' Her fingers waved in the direction of his head.

'Well, at least we're even,' Mark replied, gesturing with his head towards the swimming pool, where her garment bag was floating on the surface and making small glugging noises.

'Oh, drat,' Lexi replied and her shoulders slumped. 'There go two cocktail dresses, a business suit and a cape. The dresses I can replace, but I liked that cape.'

'A cape?' Mark repeated, strolling down the patio and picking up a long pole with a mesh net on the end.

'One of my previous clients started life as a professional magician, entertaining passengers on a cruise ship,' Lexi replied, preoccupied by watching Mark try to guide the wayward luggage to the side of the pool. Every time he got close the filter pump blew it back towards the deep end.

She winced the second time he almost had it close enough to reach.

'Fascinating man. He told me he'd kept the cape just in case he ever needed to earn a few dollars. I pointed out that after forty years in Las Vegas the chances of that happening were slim.' Lexi sniffed and gave a low chuckle. 'The rascal gave me that cape the day of the launch party for his autobiography. He'd decided that his pension didn't need boosting after all, and that at ninety-two he might be a little rusty. So we had one final performance. I was his glamorous assistant, of course. He supplied the top hat, plastic flowers and scarves. The full works. Then he patted my bottom and I threatened to cut him in half.'

She grinned. 'Happy days. It was a great party. What a shame that a vintage cape like that is going to be ruined after all of those years in showbiz…' Her eyes tracked slowly from the bag across to Mark, then back to the bag again, and she gave a dramatic sigh just to make sure that he'd got the message.

'Are you always so much trouble?' Mark asked, rolling up his trousers to reveal a surprisingly hairy pair of muscular legs before descending the steps into the shallow end of the pool and dragging the soggy garment bag onto the side.

'Oh, no,' Lexi replied in a totally casual, matter-of-fact voice as she grasped the handle and sloshed the bag farther onto the terrace, to join the other pieces of luggage she had abandoned there. 'I'm usually a lot more trouble than this. You should be grateful it was the shallow end. But these are early days.'

His reply was a snort and a brief smile illuminated his face. It was the first time she had seen Mark smile, and even in the hot afternoon sunshine she felt the warmth of it on her face. And was instantly filled with remorse.

She paused and focused on her bags before breathing out slowly, eyes down.

It was time. If she was going to do this then she had better do it now and get it over with.

Mark frowned and strolled over towards her. 'I'm sure you have enough dry clothing to last a few days. Is there something else I can help you with?'

Lexi looked up at him reluctantly and licked her lips, which were suddenly bone dry.

'Actually, there is one more thing I need to clear up

before we start working together. You see, we have met before. Just the once. In London. And not in the best of circumstances.'

She whipped off her sunglasses and hung them over the breast pocket of her jacket, looked up into his startled face.

'We weren't formally introduced at the time, but you'd just met my father in your mother's hospital room and you were rather preoccupied with escorting him out. Does that jog your memory?'

Mark paused, hands on hips, and looked at her. So they *had* met before, but…?

The hospital. Her father. Those violet-grey eyes set in a heart-shaped face.

The same eyes that had stared up at him in horror and shock after he'd punched that slimy photographer.

'Get out,' he said, cold ice reeling in his stomach, fighting the fire in his blood. 'I want you out of my house.'

'Just give me a minute,' she whispered in a hoarse, trembling voice. 'What happened that day had nothing to do with me. My father is completely out of my life. Believe me, I am only here for one reason. To do my job. As a writer.'

'Believe you? Why should I believe a single word you say? How do I know you're not here spying for your paparazzi father? No.' He shook his head, turning his back on her. 'Whoever is paying you to come here to my home has made a very grave mistake. And if you ever come near me or my family again my lawyers will be called in. Not to mention the police. So you need to leave. Right now.'

'Oh, I'll go.' She nodded. 'But I have no intention of leaving until we've cleared up some of these facts you're so fond of. Just for the record. Because I want to make something very, very clear,' she hissed through clenched teeth as she crammed every piece of clothing she could find from the soaked luggage into her handbag and vanity case.

'My parents were divorced when I was ten years old. I hadn't seen my father, the famous Mario Collazo—' she thumped the cape several times as she stuffed it farther down into the bag '—for eighteen years, until he turned up out of the blue at the clinic that morning. He'd begged my mother to give him a chance to make amends for his past mistakes and to rebuild some sort of relationship with me. And like a naive fool—' her voice softened '—no, make that a lovely, caring and heartbroken naive fool, she took the time to talk to him and actually believed him.'

Lexi shook her head and sniffed.

'She spent years sending me birthday and Christmas presents pretending that my dad still loved me. She mailed him photos and school reports every single year. And this year she'd also let him know that I was waiting for hospital treatment and asked him to come and see us when he was in London. And what did he do?'

Lexi threw her bag onto the patio floor in disgust and pressed a balled fist to each hip, well aware that she was being a drama queen but not caring a bit.

'He abused her confidence. He took advantage of a caring woman who wanted her daughter to have a relationship with her father. And she never even suspected for one moment that he'd set me up in that particular clinic on that particular day because he already knew that Crystal Leighton was going to be there.'

She lifted her chin.

'And I fell for his story just the same as she did. So if you want someone to blame for being gullible I'm right here, but I am *not* taking responsibility for what happened.'

Mark glared at her. Lexi glared back.

'Finished yet?' His voice was ice, clashing with the in-

tense fire in his eyes. The same fire she had seen once before. It had terrified her then, but she *wasn't* finished yet.

'Nowhere close. My mum is a wonderful dress designer
and wardrobe mistress. It took her years to rebuild her career after my dad left us with nothing. Her only crime—
her fault—was being too trusting, too eager to believe he'd
changed. There was no way she could have predicted he
was using her. Oh, and for the record, neither of us got
one penny of the money he got from selling those photos.
So don't you *dare* judge her. Because that is the truth—if
you're ready to accept it.'

'And what about you?' he asked, in a voice as cold as
ice. 'What's your excuse for lying to me from the moment
you arrived at the villa? You could have told me who you
were right from the start. Why didn't you? Or are *you* the
one who's unable to accept the truth?'

'Why didn't I? But I *did* tell you the truth. I stopped
being Alexis Collazo when I was sixteen years old. Oh,
yes. I changed my name on the first day that I legally
could. I *hated* the fact that my father had left my mother
and me for another woman and her daughter. I despised
him then and I think even less of him now. As far as I'm
concerned that man and his new family have nothing to do
with my life, and even less to do with my future.'

'That's ridiculous,' Mark sniped back at her, quick as
a flash. 'You can't escape the fact that your family was
involved.'

'You're right.' She nodded. 'I've had to live under the
shadow of what my father did for the last five months.
Even though I had nothing to do with it. That makes me
so angry. And most of all I hate the fact that he abused
my mother's generous, trusting spirit and used me as an
excuse to get into that hospital. If you want to go after
someone, go after him.'

'So you didn't benefit at all?'

'We got nothing—apart from the media circus when your lawyers turned up and hit us with a gagging order. Are you starting to get the picture? Good. So don't presume to judge me or my family without getting your facts straight. Because we deserve better than that.'

Mark pushed both hands deep into his trouser pockets. 'That's for me to judge,' he replied.

Lexi hoisted the suitcases upright, flung on her shoulder bag and glanced quickly around the patio before shuffling into her sandals.

'I'm finished here. If you find anything I've left behind feel free to throw it into the pool if it makes you feel better. Don't worry about the cases—I'll see myself out. Standard social politeness not required.'

'Anything to get you out of my house,' Mark replied, grabbing a suitcase in each hand as if they weighed nothing. 'Rest assured that if we should ever run into each other again, unlikely though that may be, I shall not try my best to be polite.'

'Then we understand each other perfectly,' replied Lexi. 'As far as I'm concerned, the sooner I can be back in London, the better. Best of luck writing the biography—but here's a tip.'

She hoisted her bag higher onto her shoulder and nudged her sunglasses farther up her nose.

'Perfectly happy people with perfect families living perfect lives in perfect homes don't make interesting reading. I had no idea you were my client when I came here today, but I was actually foolish enough to hope you'd be fair and listen to the truth. I even thought we might work together on this project. But it seems I was wrong about that. You won't listen to the truth if it doesn't suit you. Apparently you're just as cold, unreasonable, stubborn and controlling as the tabloids claim. I feel sorry for you.'

And with that she grabbed the vanity bag and tottered across the patio. She was already down the steps before Mark could reply.

Mark stood frozen on the patio and watched the infuriating girl teeter her way across the crazy paving, the flimsy silk dress barely covering her bottom. How dared she accuse him of being cold and stubborn? That was his father's speciality, not his. It just showed how wrong she was. How could she expect him to believe her story and put aside what he had seen with his own eyes? Mario Collazo being comforted by his daughter on the floor after Mark had knocked him down. Those were the facts.

He had recognised who she was the second she'd taken off her sunglasses. How could he forget the girl with the palest of grey eyes, filled with tears, looking up at him with such terror?

He had frightened her that morning, and in a way he regretted that. He wanted no part of his father's arrogant, bullying tactics. But at that moment he had allowed anger and rage to overwhelm him. Justifiably. It had still shocked him that he was capable of uncontrolled physical violence. He'd worked long and hard to make himself a different man from his father and his brother.

Edmund wouldn't have wasted a moment's thought before knocking any photographer to the floor and boasting about it later.

But he was *not* his older brother, the golden boy, his parents' pride and joy, who had died falling from a polo pony when he was twenty-five.

And he didn't want to be. Never had.

Mark wrapped his fingers around the handles of the

wet luggage, his chest heaving, and watched the small figure in the ridiculous outfit struggle with the door handle on the car before lowering herself onto the seat with an audible wince as her bottom connected with the hot plastic. Seconds later her legs swung inside and the door closed.

So what if she was telling the truth? What if she *had* been used by her father that day, and was just as innocent a victim as his mother had been? What if her turning up at the villa really was a total coincidence?

Then fate had just kicked them both in the teeth. And he had handed that monster an extra set of boots.

But what alternative did he have? He knew what the response would be if his father or even his sister found out that he'd been sharing precious family memories and private records with the daughter of the stalker who'd destroyed his mother's last day alive. It would be far better to forget about this fearless girl with the grey eyes and creamy skin who'd challenged him from the moment she arrived. A girl whose only crime was having the misfortune to be the daughter of a slimeball like Mario Collazo. And she had defended her mother from an attack on her reputation. In anybody else that loyalty was something he would admire.

Oh, hell!

He'd spent the last seven years of his life trying to prove that he could take his brother's place, and then his father's as head of Belmont Investments. He took risks for a living and he liked it. And now this girl turned up out of the blue and accused him of being cold and unreasonable and unwilling to listen to the truth because it didn't agree with his pre-established version of the facts.

Mark dropped both suitcases on the patio. Perfect families living perfect lives. Was that what she really thought the Belmont family was like? Perfect?

Hardly.

He looked up. The hire car hadn't moved an inch. How did she do it? How did she make him feel so angry and unsettled?

And about to make a potentially very dangerous decision.

Lexi collapsed back against the driver's seat and was about to throw her luggage onto the passenger seat when something moved inside the car. She froze, and for one fraction of a millisecond considered screaming and running back to Mark as fast as her legs could carry her.

But that would make her wimp of the week.

Hardly daring to investigate further, Lexi slowly looked sideways and blinked through her blurred vision in disbelief at the two white faces with pink ears staring back at her.

One of the kittens yawned widely, displaying the cutest little pink tongue, stretching his body out into a long curve before closing his eyes and settling down to more sleep on the sun-warmed passenger seat. The other ball of white fluff washed his face with his paw, then curled back into a matching position.

A low chuckle started deep inside her chest and rambled around for a few seconds before emerging as slightly manic strangled laughter, which soon evolved into full-blown sobbing.

Lexi closed her eyes, slumped back against the headrest and gave in to the moment. She could feel the tears running down her cheeks as the deep sobs ripped through her body, making her gasp for air. *This was not fair. This was totally not fair.*

Swallowing down her tears through a painful throat, Lexi slowly cracked open her eyes and took a firm hold of the steering wheel with both hands, curling her fingers tightly around the hot plastic as if it was a lifeline to reality.

It took a moment to realise that with all the sniffing she had not heard the gentle crunch of Mark's footsteps on the gravel driveway.

She stared straight ahead at the olive and lemon trees as he slowly strolled over to the side of the car, then leant his long tanned forearms on the open driver's window and peered inside without saying a word.

They stayed like that for a few seconds, until the silence got too much for Lexi.

'There are cats. In my car. I wasn't expecting cats in my car.' She sniffed, and then flicked down the sun visor and peered at herself in the vanity mirror.

'And look at this.' She released the steering wheel and pointed at her eyes. 'It took me an hour to put this make-up on at the airport. And now it's totally wrecked. Just like the rest of me.'

She slapped her hands down twice on the dashboard, startling the cats, who sat up and yawned at her in complaint. 'Now do you understand why I never mention my dad when I'm working? Just the mention of his name makes me all…' She waved her arms towards the windscreen and waggled her fingers about for a few seconds before dropping them into her lap.

'I noticed,' he murmured, in a calm voice tinged with just enough attention to imply that he was trying to be nice but struggling. 'And, by the way, allow me to introduce Snowy One and Snowy Two. They live here. And they tend to snuggle on warm car cushions, towels, bedding, anywhere soft and comfy. You might want to think about that when you're working outside.'

Her head slowly turned towards him so that their faces were only inches apart. And his eyes really were sky blue.

'Working?' she squeaked. 'Here?'

He nodded.

'I don't understand. A minute ago you couldn't wait to see the back of me.'

'I changed my mind.'

'Just like that?'

He nodded again.

'Have you considered the possibility that I might not want to work with you? Our last conversation was a little fraught. And I don't like being called a liar.'

'I thought about what you said.' His upper lip twitched to one side. 'And I came to the conclusion that you might have a point.'

'Oh. In that case I'm surprised it took you so long.'

Mark stared back at her with those wonderful blue eyes, and for the first time she noticed that he had the kind of positively indecent long dark eyelashes of which any mascara model would be envious.

They were so close that she could see the way the small muscles in his cheeks and jaw flexed with the suppressed tension that held his shoulders so tight, like a coiled spring.

Mark Belmont was a powder keg ready to blow, and like a fool her gentle heart actually dared to feel sorry for him. Until she remembered that he had been doing all the judging and, until now, she had been doing all the explaining.

'I'm never going to apologise, you know,' she whispered. 'Can you get past that?'

'Strange,' he replied, and the crease in his brow deepened. 'I was just about to say just the same thing. Can *you* get past that?'

'I don't know,' she replied, and took a breath before chewing on her lower lip.

Time to make her mind up. Stay and do the work or cut her losses and go. Right now.

She felt Mark's eyes scan her face, as though he were looking for some secret passage into her thoughts.

Her fingers tapped on the dashboard, but his gaze never left her face, and she could hear his breathing grow faster and faster. He was nervous, but did not want to show it. And she needed this job so badly.

'Okay,' she whispered, her eyes locked on his. 'I am going to give you another chance.'

He exhaled low and slow, and Lexi could feel his breath on her neck as the creases at the corners of his eyes warmed, distracting her for a second with the sweet heat of it. Time to get control, girl!

'Here's what's going to happen,' she continued, before Mark had a chance to answer. 'First I'm going to drag what's left of my luggage back inside your lovely villa and find a nice bedroom to sleep in. With a sea view. And then we're going to write your mother's biography to celebrate her life. And when we're finished, and it's totally and absolutely awesome and amazing, and you're standing at the book launch with your family all around you, *then* you're going to say that you couldn't possibly have created this best-seller without the help of Lexi Sloane. And that will be the end of it. No more recriminations and no more blame. Just a simple thank-you. And then we get on with our respective lives. Do you think you can do that, Mr Belmont?'

'Miss Sloane…'

'Yes?' she muttered, wondering what conditions and arguments he was going to wrap around her proposal.

'My cat has just peed on your shoe.'

She looked down just as Snowy One shook his left leg

and then clawed his way back onto the car seat without the slightest whiff of contrition.

'Can I take that as a yes?' she huffed.

'Absolutely.'

CHAPTER FOUR

M<small>ARK</small> woke just as the morning sunlight hit that one perfect angle where it was able to slant around the edge of
the blackout blind and shine a laser beam straight onto
his pillow.

He groaned and blinked several times, turning to glance
at the wristwatch he wore 24/7. It was set to tell the time
in each of the main financial markets as well as local time
on Paxos. And at that moment they were all screaming the
same thing. He had slept for a grand total of four hours
since forcing himself into bed at dawn.

By 9:00 a.m. on a normal weekday Mark would already
have showered, dressed, had breakfast and coffee and been
at his desk for three hours. Insomnia had been his faith-
ful companion for years—he'd hoped that being back on
Paxos would help him to catch up on his sleep.

Wrong again.

Pushing himself up on the bed, which was a total wreck,
Mark reached across to his bedside table for his glasses and
tablet computer and quickly checked through the emails
his PA had filtered for him. London was an hour behind
Paxos, but the financial markets waited for no man and his
team started early and worked late. They earned the huge
salaries he paid them to make Belmont Investments one
of the most respected London financial houses.

Ten minutes later he'd sent replies to emails that needed his personal attention and forwarded others to the heads of department to action.

Then he turned to the real nightmare. The restructuring plans which would secure the long-term stability and profitability of the company. It was going to be tough convincing his father that these difficult measures needed to be taken, and they had already been delayed for months following his mother's death and his father's illness.

But the real problem was his father. He had built up Belmont Investments by taking a low-key, low-risk approach that had worked well years ago. Not any longer. Not in today's financial market.

Mark flicked over to his own plan—the plan he'd been working on in the early hours of the morning when sleep had been impossible. It was dynamic, modern and exciting, and until now this plan had been a dirty secret that he hadn't shared with anyone else.

His father would hate it. But he had to do something to save the business. Even if it meant breaking through the unwritten rules his father had laid down—rules which came with all the obligations attached to being the next Baron Belmont.

Mark quickly scanned through one of the key implementation plans, and had just started to work on the projected time schedule, looking for ways to bring it forward, when he heard strange, cooing baby-love sounds below his bedroom window.

And they were definitely human.

Mark closed his eyes, dropping the tablet onto his knees with a low sigh.

Of course. Just for a second he'd forgotten about his uninvited and very unexpected houseguest. Miss Alexis Sloane.

No doubt fresh as a daisy, bursting with energy, and ready to get started on ripping his family history apart so she could collect her fee and head back to civilisation as fast as her cute, shapely and very lovely little legs could carry her.

A whisper of doubt crept into his mind.

What if he had made a mistake when he'd asked her to stay?

What if this was all some elaborate ruse and Lexi truly was intending to leave with all the Belmont family secrets tucked under her arm, neatly packed up to pass on to her paparazzi father?

For all Mark knew he could be handing Mario Collazo all the ammunition he needed to twist Crystal Leighton's life story into some sordid tabloid hatchet-job.

He slipped out of bed and padded over to the window to peek out onto the patio.

Lexi was bending down and was rubbing her fingers together in front of Emmy and Oscar, the feral cats who called this villa home and whose kittens had invaded her car. The cats clearly couldn't decide whether this replacement for Mark's soft-hearted housekeeper was friend or foe, and were taking the 'feed me and I'll think about it' approach. But at least she was making an effort to be friendly.

Mark almost snorted out loud. He'd made the mistake of bringing his one-time fiancée here for a weekend break. She'd been horrified that he allowed 'vermin' so close to the house, and actively shooed the cats away at every opportunity in case they contaminated her clothing—which had confused Emmy and Oscar so much that they'd kept coming back to find out what was going on.

She'd lasted three days before stage-managing an emergency at the bank.

Pity he hadn't picked up on the clue that the beautiful girl had enjoyed the kudos of being the future Baroness Belmont a lot more than she'd liked him and his ordinary life.

He pulled back the blind just an inch and watched Lexi dangle a piece of ribbon up and down, inviting the cats to play with this strange new toy. Her childlike laughter rang out in the sunshine and was so infectious that he couldn't help but smile in return.

It struck him all at once that his life revolved around people who were very different from the girl he was looking at now. Lexi was pretty, dynamic and confident enough to challenge him and defend herself against what she saw as unfair treatment.

If this was an act, then she was playing her part very well indeed.

The girl he was looking at—okay, ogling—seemed to have no off button. No dial he could turn to slow her down and make her start conforming a little to other people's expectations.

She had surprised him by telling him who her father was before they'd started work.

A shrewder person might have kept quiet about that little bombshell until the cheque had cleared.

Honesty and integrity. He admired that. Even if she *was* the daughter of a man he despised. And, unless he had lost his knack of judging people, she was telling the truth about not knowing she'd be working with Mark.

Overall, a fascinating, intriguing and very unsettling package. Who probably didn't realise that as she bent over the back of her hipster slim-fit trousers, which were probably extremely fashionable in the city, had slid way down past her hips, exposing the top of what passed for her underwear. And providing him with a splendid and tantalising view of a smooth expanse of skin divided by a tiny band of what appeared to be red lace.

Considering the hot weather, and the tightness of her trousers, it was just about as uncomfortable and unsuitable a combination as he could imagine.

But if her intention was to make a man's heart pound rather too fast, she had succeeded brilliantly.

She was skipping across the patio now, perilously close to the swimming pool where he had held her so close against his body—and had enjoyed every second of it. Enjoyed it rather too much for comfort.

That was it. She made him feel…uncomfortable.

Of course that had been until he'd looked into those remarkable violet-grey eyes and instantly been transported back to the horror of that morning in a London clinic when his world had collapsed around him. And that was not uncomfortable. It was damning.

Mark released the blind and took off his glasses.

Perhaps it was just as well that he knew who her family were. She was way too attractive to ignore, but that was as far as it went—as far as it could ever go.

There was no way around it. Lexi Sloane was part of his past. The question was, would she be able to help him get through this project so he could move on to his future?

Because if he had made the wrong choice, then bringing Lexi into his life could be the worst decision he'd ever made.

Lexi sang along under her breath to the lively trance track blasting her eardrums while she flicked through her cellphone messages, sending off fast replies to the most urgent and deleting what she could.

She was just about to switch to emails when Adam sent her yet another text. That had to be the fourth in the last twenty-four hours.

Please. Call me. We need to talk.

'Oh, I don't think so, loser. You don't tell me what to do. Not any more,' Lexi hissed, moving on to the next message. But the damage was done: her eyes and brain refused to connect and she put down the phone in disgust.

The last time they had spoken face to face had been in the hall of Adam's apartment. Both of them had said things which could not be unsaid. And then she had embarrassed herself by slapping him harder than she'd ever hit anything in her life.

Girls did that when they found out their boyfriends had been cheating on them.

What a fool she'd been to pin all her hopes of happiness on the one man she'd thought was a friend. She should have learned from her mother's experience not to let personal feelings interfere with her judgement. And that was exactly what she'd done. Stupid girl.

She wasn't going to live in Gullible Girl City again. Oh, no. At least not until her home office was ready and her children's books were in the shops.

Then she might think about dating again. If...

She held the thought as she caught a blur of movement in the corner of her eye and turned her head just as Mark strolled into the room. He was wearing loose navy trousers and a very expensive-looking navy polo shirt. His hair was dark and slick, as though he had just stepped out of the shower.

Mark Belmont looked like heaven on legs.

And with one single glance she was instantly hit with a sudden attack of the killer tingles.

The kind of tingles that left a girl feeling hot, bothered, brainless and desperate enough to do something really stupid. Like forgetting that Mark was her client. Like wanting to find out what it felt like to run her fingers through his hair and feel his breath on her neck.

Bad tingles. *Very* bad tingles.

Not ideal qualities for a professional writer.

This was the man who'd accused her of being her father's accomplice and almost thrown her out yesterday. As far as Mark Belmont was concerned she was here to work. And that was all. She had to keep her head together!

It was time to turn on a cheery nonsense gossipy voice and the fixed smile that had become her standard mask to the world. Busy, busy, busy. Chatter, chatter, chatter. That was the role she played. He wouldn't be able to get a word in edgeways, and she could keep her distance.

Deep breath. Cue, Lexi. Action!

'Good morning, Mr Belmont.' She smiled, nervously rearranging the cutlery to hide her complete mental disarray. 'I hope you're ready for breakfast, since I've been on a mission of mercy and made the village baker and shopkeeper very happy. But please don't be worried about your reputation as a ladies' man. I told them I was only here for a few days to help with a business project and I'd be heading back to the office ASAP.'

Oh, and now she was babbling about his love life. Great. Could she be more pathetic?

'My reputation?' Mark repeated, staring at her through those incredibly cute spectacles as he leant against the worktop, his hands in his trouser pockets. Casual, handsome, devastating. 'How very thoughtful of you. But why did you think it necessary to go on a mission of mercy?'

'I was brave enough to rummage around inside your freezer looking for breakfast. Behind the bags of ice cubes were a few ancient, dry bread rolls, which crumbled to pieces in my hands and were only fit for the birds, and an assortment of unlabelled mystery items which, judging by their greyish-green colour, were originally of biological origin. But they did have one thing in common. They were all inedible.'

She stopped cutting bread and looked up into Mark's face. 'It's amazing what they have in small village shops on this island.'

'Food shopping,' he replied, running the fingers of one hand through his damp hair. 'Ah. Yes. My housekeeper stocked up the refrigerator last week, but of course I wasn't expecting visitors.'

'No need to apologise,' she said as brightly as she could. 'But it has been my experience that we can get a lot more work done if we have food available in the house and don't have to run out and stock up at the last minute. And, since the room service around here seems to be a little deficient, some creative thinking was required.'

He peered over her shoulder and the smell of citrus shower gel and coconut shampoo wafted past. She inhaled the delicious combination, which was far more enticing than the food and did absolutely nothing to cure her attack of the tingles.

But as he stepped forward Lexi heard his stomach growl noisily and raised her eyebrows at him.

'It seems that I *could* use some breakfast. Um… What did you manage to scavenge?'

'Since I don't know if you prefer a sweet chocolatey cereal breakfast or a savoury eggs, bacon and tomatoes type breakfast, I bought both. I've already had scrambled eggs and toast, washed down with a gallon of tea.'

'Tea is disgusting. But eggs and toast sound perfect if I can persuade you to go back to the frying pan. I'll take care of my coffee. It's one of my few weaknesses. I'm very particular about what coffee I drink, where it came from and how it was made.'

'Of course, Mr Belmont,' Lexi replied, with no hint of sarcasm in her voice, and turned back towards the cooker.

'It's Mark.'

'Oh,' she replied, whizzing round towards him and making a point of taking out her earphones. 'Did you say something?'

Mark crossed his arms and narrowed his eyes, well aware that she had heard what he said but was making a play of it since she had just scored a point. 'I said, since we will be working together, I would prefer it if you called me Mark.'

'If that is your instruction, Mr Belmont.' She smiled and relaxed a little. 'I'd be very happy to call you Mark. But only if you call me Lexi in return. Not Alexis, or Ali, or Lex, but Lexi.'

Then she turned back to the hob and added a knob of butter to the hot pan before breaking more eggs into a bowl.

'Breakfast will be with you in about five minutes, Mark. I do hope you like orange juice. That was the only—'

The sound of a rock band belted out from her cell phone, and Lexi quickly wiped her hands on a kitchen towel before pressing a few buttons.

'Anything interesting?' Mark asked casually as he reached for the coffee.

'I always receive interesting messages.' Lexi twisted to one side and peered at the display. 'But in this case they were two new messages from my ex-boyfriend, which are now deleted. Unread, of course. Which I find deeply satisfying.'

'I see. I thought you might be a heartbreaking sort of girl.'

'It cannot be denied. But in this particular situation it transpired he was cheating on me with a girl who took great satisfaction in enticing him away from me.'

Mark's eyebrows went skywards and his lips did a strange quivery dance as his hands stilled on the cafetière. 'He cheated on you?' he repeated in an incredulous voice, then shook his head once before going back to his coffee. 'Do you always share details of your fascinating-but-tragic love life with people you've only just met?' he asked with a quick glance in her direction.

Lexi shrugged, and was about to make some dismissive quip when it struck her that he was actually trying to have a conversation this morning.

That was different.

He'd barely said a word over their light dinner of crackers, cheese and sweet tomatoes apart from commenting on the local red wine. The meal had been so awkward that she'd felt she was walking on eggshells every time she tried to break the silence.

She wasn't complaining, and it helped that she now wasn't the only one talking, but she wasn't used to having one-to-one, intelligent, hangover-free conversations with her clients at this time in the morning. Perhaps Mark Belmont had a few more surprises for her?

'Oh, yes,' Lexi replied with a shrug as she added lightly beaten eggs to the sizzling butter in the pan and immediately started working the mix. 'But, if you think about it, my job is to help *you* share details of *your* fascinating-but-tragic love life with strangers whom *you* are never

going to meet. This way we are both in the same business.
I think it works.'

'Ah.' Mark pressed his lips together and gave Lexi
a small nod as he carried the coffee over to the table.
'Good point. I should probably tell you that I am not totally thrilled by that prospect.'

'I understand that. Not everyone is a natural extrovert.'
She shrugged just as the bread popped up from the toaster.
'But that's why you called me in.'

'I prefer keeping my private life just that. Private. I
would much rather stick to the facts.'

'Are you speaking from past experience?' Lexi asked
quietly, flashing him a lightning-quick glance as she
quickly tipped hot scrambled egg onto a thick slice of
golden toast.

'Perhaps it is,' Mark replied between sips of juice. 'And
perhaps it isn't.'

'I see.' Lexi slid the plate onto the table. 'Well, I can tell
you one thing. If you want this biography to work you're
going to have to trust me and get that private life out for
the world to see, Mark.'

His response was a close-mouthed frown which spoke
volumes.

Oh, this was turning out so well.

Lexi nodded towards the food. 'Enjoy your breakfast.
Then I really do need to find out how much work you've
done so far on the manuscript. Perhaps you could show
me your mother's study? That'd be a good place to start.
In the meantime I'm off to feed the cats. Bye.'

And Lexi waltzed out of the kitchen diner on her wedge
sandals, safe in the knowledge that Mark's stunned blue
eyes were burning holes in her spectacular back.

CHAPTER FIVE

LEXI followed Mark through a door to a large room on the first floor, looking around in delight and awe.

Crystal Leighton had not had a study. Crystal Leighton had created a private library.

'How did you know my mother even had a study? I don't recall mentioning it.'

Lexi touched two fingers to her forehead in reply to Mark's question. 'Intuition. Combined with the number of rooms in this huge house and the fact that Crystal Leighton was an undisputed artist. Any creative person coming to this island would bring a fine collection of writing materials and reading matter with them. And when it's your own house… She would have a study. Elementary, my dear Watson.' She tapped her nose and winked in his direction. 'But this…' she continued, whistling softly and waving her arm around the room, turning from side to side in delight. 'This is…wonderful.'

'You like it?'

'*Like* it?' She blinked at him several times. 'This is heaven. I could stay here all day and night and never come up for air. Total bliss! I love books. Always have. In fact I cannot remember a time when I haven't had a book to hand.'

She almost jogged across the room and started poring

through the contents of the bookcases. 'Poetry, classics, philosophy, history, languages. Blockbuster fiction?' She flashed him a glance and he shrugged.

'I have a sister.'

'Ah, fair enough. We all need some relaxing holiday reading. But look at this collection of screenplays and books on the theatre. My mother would be so envious. Did I mention that she works as a wardrobe mistress? She loves reading about the theatre.'

'Every school holiday my mother used to stuff a spare suitcase with plays, books, scripts her agent had sent— anything that caught her eye.' Mark gave a faint smile and plunged his hands into his trouser pockets, nodding towards the shelves. 'I spent many wet and windy afternoons in this room.'

'I envy you that. And it's just what I need.' Lexi turned to face Mark, resting her fingertips lightly on the paper-strewn table in the centre of the room. 'Have you ever heard the expression that you can tell a lot about someone from the books they have in their home? It's true. You can.'

'I'm not so sure about that,' Mark replied with a dismissive grunt. 'What about the car magazines, polo-pony manuals and the school textbooks on biochemistry?'

She shook her head and waved with one hand at three particular shelves. 'Theatre history and set design. Fashion photography. Biographies of the Hollywood greats. Don't you see? That combination screams out the same message. Crystal Leighton was an intelligent professional actress who understood the importance of image and design. And that's the message we should be aiming for. Professional excellence. What do you think?'

'Think? I haven't had time to think,' Mark replied, and inhaled deeply, straightening his back so that Lexi felt as though he was towering over her. 'My publisher may have arranged your contract, but I'm still struggling with the idea of sharing personal family papers and records with someone I don't know. This is very personal to me.'

'You're a private person who doesn't like being rail-roaded. I get that. And I can understand that you're still not sure about my reason for being here in the first place.' She glanced up at his startled face and gave a small snort. 'It's okay, Mark. I'm not a spy for the paps. Never have been. No plans to be one any time soon. And if I was stalking you I would have told you.'

Lexi turned sideways away from the table and ran her fingers across the spines of the wonderful books on the shelves. 'Here's an idea. You're worried about sharing your family secrets with a stranger. Let's change that. What do you want to know about me? Ask me anything. Anything at all. And I'll tell you the truth.'

'Anything? Okay, let's start with the obvious. Why bi-ographies? Why not write fiction or business books?'

She paused and licked her lips, but kept her eyes focused on the books in front of her. To explain properly she would have to reveal a great deal of herself and her history. That could be difficult. But she'd made a pact with herself. No lies, no deception. Just go with it. Even if her life seemed like a sad joke compared to Mark's perfect little family.

'Just after my tenth birthday I was diagnosed with a se-rious illness and spent several months in hospital.'

'I'm so sorry,' he whispered after a few seconds of total silence.

She sensed him move gently forward and lean against the doorframe so that he was looking at her.

'That must have been awful for you and your parents.'

She nodded. 'Pretty bad. My parents were going through

a rough time as it was, and I knew my father had a pathological hatred of hospitals. Ironic, huh?' She smiled at him briefly, still half-lost in the recollection. 'Plus, he was working in America at the time. The problem was, he didn't come home for a couple of months, and when he did he brought his new girlfriend with him.'

'Oh, no.' Mark's eyebrows went north but his tense shoulders went south.

'Oh, *yes*. I spent the first year recovering at my grandmother's house on the outskirts of London, with a very miserable mother and even more miserable grandmother. It was not the happiest of times, but there was one consolation that kept me going. My grandmother was a wonderful storyteller, and she made sure that I was supplied with books of every shape and form. I loved the children's stories, of course, but the books I looked for in the public library told of how other people had survived the most horrific of early lives and still came through smiling.'

'Biographies. You liked reading other people's life stories.'

'Could not get enough.' She nodded once. 'Biographies were my favourite. It didn't take long for me to realise that autobiographies are tricky things. How can you be objective about your own life and what you achieved at each stage? The biography, on the other hand, is something completely different: it's someone else telling you about a mysterious and fabulous person. They can be incredibly personal, or indifferent and cold. Guess what kind I like?'

'So you decided to become a writer?' Mark asked. 'That was a brave decision.'

'Perhaps. I had the chance to go to university but I couldn't afford it. So I went to work for a huge publishing house in London who released more personal life stories every year than all of the other publishers put together.'

She grinned up at Mark. 'It was *amazing.* Two years later I was an assistant editor, and the rest, as they say, is history.'

She reached her right hand high into the air and gave him a proper, over-the-top, twirling bow. 'Ta-da. And that's it. That's how I got into this crazy, outrageous business.' Lexi looked up at him coquettishly through her eyelashes as she stood up. 'Now. Anything else you'd like to know before we get started?'

'Only one thing. Why are you wearing so much make-up at nine o'clock in the morning? On a small Greek island? In fact, make that *any* island?

Lexi chuckled, straightening up to her full height, her head tilted slightly to one side.

'I take it as a compliment that you even noticed, Mark. This is my job, and this is my work uniform. Office, movie studio, pressroom or small Greek island. It doesn't make any difference. Putting on the uniform takes me straight into my working head—which is what you're paying me for. So, with that in mind, let's make a start.'

Lexi pulled down several books from the shelves and stacked them in front of Mark.

'There are as many different types of biography as there are authors. By their nature each one is unique and special, and should be matched to the personality of the person they are celebrating. Light or serious, respectful or challenging. It depends on what you want to say and how you want to say it. Which one of these do you like best?'

Mark exhaled loudly. 'I had no idea this would be so difficult. Or so complex.'

Lexi picked up a large hardback book with a photograph of a distinguished theatre actor on the cover and passed it to Mark.

She sighed as Mark flicked through the pages of small,

tightly written type with very little white space. 'They can also be terribly dry, because the person writing is trying their hardest to be respectful while being as comprehensive as possible. There are only so many times an actor can play Hamlet and make each performance different. Lists of who did what, when and where are brilliant for an appendix to the book—but they don't tell you about the *person,* about their *soul.'*

'Do you know I actually met this actor a couple of times at my mother's New Year parties?' Mark waved the book at Lexi before dropping it back to the table with a loud thump. 'For a man who had spent fifty years in the theatre he was actually very shy. He much preferred one-to-one conversations to holding centre stage like some of his fellow actors did.'

'Exactly!' Lexi leant forward, animated. 'That's what a biographer *should* be telling us about. How did this shy man become an international award-winning actor who got stage fright every single night in his dressing room but still went out there and gave the performance of his life for the audience? That's what we want to know. That's how you do justice to the memory of the remarkable person you are writing about. By sharing real and very personal memories that might have nothing to do with the public persona at all but can tell the reader everything about who that person truly was and what it meant to have them in your life. That's the gold dust.'

Mark frowned. 'So it all has to be private revelations?'

'Not all *revelations.* But there has to be an intimacy, a connection between reader and subject—not just lists of dry facts and dates.' Lexi shrugged. 'It's the only way to be true to the person you're writing about. And that's why you should be excited that you have this opportunity to make your mother come alive to a reader through your book. Plus, your publisher will love you for it.'

'Excited? That's not quite the word I was thinking of.'

She rubbed her hands together and narrowed her eyes. 'I think it's time for you to show me what you've done so far. Then we can talk about your memories and personal stories which will make this book better than you ever thought possible.'

Lexi sat down at the table, her eyes totally focused on the photographs and yellowing newspaper clippings spilling out of an old leather suitcase.

Mark strolled towards her, cradling his coffee cup, but as she looked up towards him her top slipped down a fraction and he was so entranced by the tiny tattoo of a blue butterfly on her shoulder that he forgot what he was about to say.

'Now, I'm going to take a leap here, but would it be fair to say that you haven't actually made much progress on the biography itself? Actual words on paper? Am I right?'

'Not quite,' Mark replied, stepping away to escape the tantalisingly smooth creaminess of Lexi's bare shoulder and elegant neck. 'My mother started working on a book last summer when she was staying here, and she wrote several chapters about her earlier life as well as pulling together those bundles of papers over there. But that's about it. And her handwriting was always pretty difficult to decipher.'

'Oh, that's fine.'

'Fine?' he replied, lifting his chin. 'How can it possibly be *fine?* I have two weeks to get this biography into shape, or I miss the deadline and leave it to some hack to spill the usual tired old lies and make more money out of my mother's death.' Mark picked up a photograph of Crystal Leighton, the movie star, at the height of her career. 'Have you any idea how angry that makes me? They think they know her because of the movies she worked on. They haven't got a clue.'

He shook his head and shuffled the photograph back into the same position, straightening the edges so that each of the clippings and photographs were exactly aligned in a neat column down one side. 'I don't expect you to understand how important this biography is to me, but she is not here to defend herself any more. Now that's my job.'

Lexi stared at Mark in silence for a moment, the air between them bristling with tension and anxiety.

How could she make him understand that she knew exactly what it was like to live two lives? People envied her her celebrity lifestyle, the constant travel, the vibrancy and excitement of her work. They had no clue whatsoever that under the happy, chatty exterior was a girl doing everything she could to fight off the despair of her life. Her desperate need to have children and a family of her own, and the sure knowledge that it was looking less and less likely ever to happen. Adam had been her best chance. And now he was gone... Oh, yes, she knew about acting a part.

'You think I don't understand? Oh, Mark, how very wrong you are. I know only too well how hard it is to learn to live with that kind of pain.'

She watched as he inhaled deeply before replying. 'How stupid and selfish of me,' he said eventually in a low voice. 'I sometimes forget that other people have lost family members and survived. It was especially insensitive after what you've just been telling me about your father.'

'Oh, it happens in the very best of families,' she said with a sad smile. 'Your mother died a few months ago, while I've had almost twenty years to work through the fact that my father abandoned us. And that pain does not go away.'

'You sound very resigned—almost forgiving. I'm not sure I could be.'

'Then I'm a very good actress. I've never forgiven him and I don't know if I ever can. A girl has to know her limitations, and this is one of mine. Not going to happen. Can we move on?'

Lexi looked up into Mark's eyes as she asked the question, just as he looked into hers. And in the few seconds of complete silence that followed something clicked across the electrically charged space between them.

'And just when I thought you were perfection,' he whispered, in a voice which was so rich and low and seductive that the tingles went into overdrive.

Lexi casually formed the fingers of both her hands into a tent shape, raised an eyebrow and stared at him through the triangular gap between her fingers.

'There you have it. I have flaws, after all. You must be incredibly disappointed that a respectable agency sent you a defective ghost writer. You should ask for a discount immediately. And I shall officially hand back my halo and declare myself human and fallible.'

Mark smiled. 'I rather like the idea. Perhaps there *is* hope for the rest of us?'

'Really? In that case,' she breathed in a low, hoarse voice, 'let's talk about your baby photos.'

And Mark immediately swallowed the wrong way and sprayed coffee all over his school reports.

They had hardly stopped for over three hours. He had made coffee. Lexi had made suggestions, dodging back and forth to the kitchen to bring snacks.

And, together, somehow they had sorted out the huge

suitcase bursting with various pieces of paper and photographs that he had brought with him from London into two stacks, roughly labelled as either 'career' or 'home life.' A cardboard box was placed in the middle for anything which had to be sorted out later.

And his head was bursting with frustration, unease and unbridled admiration.

Lexi was not only dedicated and enthusiastic, but she possessed such a natural delight and genuine passion for discovering each new aspect of his mother's life and experience that it was infectious. It was as though every single scrap of trivia was a precious item of buried treasure—an ancient artefact that deserved to be handled with the ultimate care and pored over in meticulous detail.

It had been Lexi's idea to start sorting the career stack first, so she knew the scope and complexity of the project right from the start.

Just standing next to her, trying to organise newspaper clippings and press releases into date order, made him feel that they might *just* be able to create some order out of the magpie's nest of thirty years' worth of memorabilia.

He couldn't remember most of the movie events that his mother had attended when he was a boy, so photographs from the red carpet were excellent markers—and yet, for him, they felt totally repetitive. Another pretty dress. Another handsome male lead. Yet another interview with the same newspaper. Saying the same things over and over again.

But Lexi saw each image in a completely different way. Every time she picked a photograph up she seemed to give a tiny gasp of delight. Every snippet of gossip about the actors and their lives, or the background to each story, was new and fresh and exciting in her eyes. Each line provided a new insight into the character of the woman who'd been a leading lady in the USA and in the British movie and TV world for so many years that she had practically become an institution.

Dates, names, public appearances, TV interviews—everything was recorded and checked against the film-company records through the power of the internet, then tabulated in date order, creating a miraculous list which they both agreed might not be totally complete, but gave the documented highlights.

And from this tiny table, in this small villa on Paxos, in only three hours, they had managed to create a potted history of his mother's movie career. All backed up by photographs and paper records. Ready to use, primed to create a timeline for the acting life of Crystal Leighton.

Which was something very close to amazing.

He wondered if Lexi realised that when she was reading intently she tapped her pen against her chin and pushed her bottom lip out in a sensuous pout, and sometimes she started humming a pop tune under her breath—before realising what she was doing and turning it into a chuckle because it had surprised her.

Every time she walked past him her floral fragrance seemed to reach out towards him and draw him closer to her, like a moth to a flame. It was totally intoxicating, totally overwhelming. And yet he hadn't asked her to wash it off. That would have been rude.

The problem was, working so closely together around such a small table meant that their bodies frequently touched. Sleeve on sleeve, leg on leg—or, in his case, long leg against thigh.

And at that moment, almost as though she'd heard his

innermost thoughts, Lexi lifted up the first folder of the second stack and brushed his arm with her wrist. That small contact was somehow enough to set his senses on fire.

Worse, a single colour photograph slipped out from between the pages and fell onto the desk. Two boys grinned back at Mark from the matte surface—the older boy proud and strong, chin raised, his arm loosely draped across the back and shoulder of his younger brother, who was laughing adoringly at the person taking the photograph.

Mark remembered the football match at boarding school as though it were yesterday. Edmund had scored two goals and been made man of the match. Nothing new there. Except that for once in his life nerdy Mark Belmont had come out from the wings and sailed the ball past the head of the goalkeeper from a rival school.

And, best of all, his mother had seen him score the winning goal and taken the photograph. She had always made time in her schedule if she could to attend school sports days.

Edmund had called him a show-off, of course. And maybe he'd been right. Mark had wanted to prove to at least one of his parents that he could be sporty when he wanted.

He inhaled slowly through his nose, but just as Lexi stretched her hand out towards the photograph he picked it up and pushed it back on the pile.

Not now. He was not ready to do that. Not yet.

But there was no escaping his companion's attention to detail. Lexi instantly dived into the stack and retrieved the photograph.

'Is this your brother?' she asked.

He took a moment and gave a quick nod. 'Yes. Edmund was eighteen months older than me. This was taken at our boarding school. The Belmont boys had just scored all three of the goals. We were the heroes of the hour...' His voice trailed away.

Out of the corner of his eye he realised that she was standing quite silent and still. Until then it hadn't dawned on him that her body was usually in constant motion. Her hands, shoulders and hips had been jiggling around every second of the day, which was probably why she was so slender. This girl lived on adrenaline.

But not now. Now she was just waiting—waiting for him to tell her about Edmund.

He picked up the photograph and gently laid it to the far right of the table. Recent history. Too recent as far as he was concerned.

'He died seven years ago in a polo accident in Argentina.'

If he was expecting revulsion, or some snide comment, he was wrong. Instead Lexi gently laid her fingertips on the back of his hand in a fleeting moment of total compassion. And he felt every cell of his skin open up and welcome her in.

'Your poor mother,' Lexi whispered, only inches away from him.

He turned his head slightly. Her eyes were scanning his face as if she was looking for something and not finding it.

'That must have been so heartbreaking. I can't imagine what it's like to raise a child to manhood and then lose him.'

Her gaze slid down his face and focused on a family snap of his mother. Not a studio press release or a publicity shot. This was a photo he had taken with his pocket camera when his mother had been manning the cake stall at a local garden fête. She was wearing a simple floral tea dress with a white daisy from the garden stuck behind one ear. But what made her really beautiful was the totally natural expression of happiness she wore.

It was just as hard as he'd thought it might be, look-ing at the photograph and remembering her laughing and chatting and waving at him to put down the camera and enjoy himself.

Lexi ran a fingertip ever so gently across the surface of the print. He steeled himself, ready to answer her question about how the famous actress Crystal Leighton had come to be working behind the counter of a country village fête.

That was why, when she did ask a question, it knocked him slightly off-balance.

'How old is your sister?

'Cassie? Twenty-seven,' he replied, puzzled. 'Why do you ask?'

'Because I'm going to need to talk to her about Edmund. I know she's a lot younger, but I'm sure she can remember her eldest brother very clearly.'

'So can I,' he retorted. 'We were at school together— more like twins than brothers.'

'And that's the point. You're too close. You can't pos-sibly be objective, and I wouldn't expect you to be. He was your best friend and then you lost him—and that's hard. I'm so sorry. You must miss him terribly,' she whis-pered, and her teeth started to gnaw on her full lower lip in distress.

The deep shudder came from within his chest, and it must have been so loud that Lexi heard it. Because she smiled a half smile of understanding and regret and looked away. As though she was giving him a moment to com-pose himself.

Just the thought of that generous gesture flicked a switch inside his head that went from the calm controlled setting straight to the righteous anger mode.

This woman, this *stranger* who had walked into his life

less than twenty-four hours earlier, was giving him a moment to bring his pain back under control.

Nothing she could have done would have made him more furious.

How *dared* she presume that he was unable to control himself?

That he was unable to do the job he had set himself because of the foolish, sensitive emotions in the gentle heart he had suppressed for all these years?

He'd learned the hard way that the Belmont men did not talk about Edmund and how his death had wrenched them apart. No. Instead they were expected to shoulder the extra responsibilities and obligations and carry on as though Edmund had never existed.

Lexi pressed both hands flat against the table, lifted her head and looked into his eyes.

And, to Mark's horror, he saw the glint of moisture at the corners of her own eyes—which were not violet after all, he realised, but more of a grey colour in the diffused warm light coming in through the cream-lace curtains from the sunny garden outside. Her eyelashes were not black, like his, but dark brown, with a tint of copper. The same colour as her hair—well, most of it. The places that weren't streaked with purple highlights.

But it was those amazing eyes that captivated him and dragged him helplessly into their depths. Multiple shades of grey and violet with blue speckles gazed back at him, with the black centres growing darker and wider as her eyes locked onto his and refused to let go. And he simply could not look away.

Those were the same eyes that had stared up at him in total horror that morning in the hospital. The same eyes that were now brimming with compassion and warmth and delight. And he had never seen anything like it before.

His mother had used to say that eyes were the windows to the heart.

And if that was true then Lexi Sloane had a remarkable heart.

But the fact remained—just looking into those eyes took him back to a place which shouted out, loud and clear, one single overpowering word.

Failure.

He had failed to protect his mother.

He had failed to replace Edmund.

He had let his parents down and was still letting them down.

And just the sight of his mother's pretty face looking back at him from all these photographs was like a knife to the heart.

'How do you do it?' he demanded through clenched teeth. 'How do you do this job for a living? Poring over the pain and suffering of other people's lives? Do you get some sick pleasure out of it? Or do you use other people's pain in order to make your own life feel better and safer in some way? Please tell me, because I don't understand. I just don't.'

He was trembling now, and so annoyed by his own lack of self-control that he brusquely slipped his hand out from under hers, turned away and strode downstairs to the patio doors, pulled them open sharply and stepped outside onto the cool shaded terrace.

Well, that was clever. Well done, Mark. Very slick. Taking your problems out on the nearest person, just like your dad would.

He closed his eyes and fought to control his breathing. Minutes seemed to stretch into hours until he heard the gentle tapping of Lexi's light footsteps on the tile floor behind him.

She came and stood next to him at the railing, so that they were both looking out across the pool towards the cypress trees and olive groves in total silence.

'I don't do this job out of some sick pleasure or self-gratification. Well…' she shrugged '…apart from the fact that I get paid, of course. No. I do it to help my clients record how they came through the traumas of their lives to become the person they are now. And that's what other people want to read about.' She half turned at the railing. 'I was serious when I told you how much I loved reading about other people's lives. I love meeting people. I love hearing their life stories.'

Her fingers tapped on the varnished wood. 'Just in case you haven't noticed, every family in this world suffers pain and loss, and every single person—every one—has to survive horrible trauma which changes their lives forever. That includes me, you and all our families and friends. There is no escape. It's how we deal with it that makes us who we are. That's all.'

'That's *all?*' He shook his head. 'When did *you* become an expert in sorting out other people's lives and their histories for them? You're hardly perfect yourself—not with *your* father.'

The temperature of the air dropped ten degrees, and the icy blast hit Mark hard on the forehead and woke him up.

He hadn't meant to sound bitter or cruel, but suppressed emotion and tiredness swept over him like a wave and he needed a few moments before he could very, very slowly relax his manic hold on the railing and start to breathe again. He was only too aware that Lexi was watching his every move in silence.

'I apologise for that outburst, Miss Sloane. It was uncalled for and unnecessary. I thought that we could get past what happened at the hospital but apparently I was mistaken. I can quite understand if you would prefer not to work with me after my rudeness. In fact, if you pack your bags now, you should be able to catch the ferry which leaves at four. I'll make sure your hire car is picked up at the harbour, and that the agency pays your full fee. Thank you for your help this morning.'

CHAPTER SIX

Lᴇxɪ stared at him as the hot sun beat down on her shoulders.

Yesterday Mark had listened to the truth about her father and still given her a chance to work with him. Now he had thrown her heritage back in her face—and then apologised to her for it.

He was the most contrary, annoying and confusing man she had met in a long time. But under that bravado something told her that he was okay. Intensely private, ambushed into having her at his house, but okay.

And she was not giving up on him.

'Oh, I'm well aware that I am very far from perfect. Stubborn, too. Put those two things together and the result is that I'm not going anywhere,' she replied with a lilting voice, and raised both hands, palms forward. 'This happens all the time. Who in their right mind wants to talk about the pain of the past? It's human nature to push all this turmoil into a box and lock the lid down tight so we can get on with our daily lives.'

And I should know.

She glanced from side to side, but the only living creatures within sight were the four cats along the wall. 'I'm not allowed to talk about other clients, because those confidentiality agreements I sign are completely watertight, but believe me—I've worked with some people and I don't know how they get through the day with all the baggage they're carrying. I thought I had problems until I worked with *real* survivors.'

'Is that what we are? Survivors?'

'Every single one of us. Every day. And there's nothing we can do about it. Although I do know one thing.'

He slowly exhaled. 'I can hardly wait to hear it.'

'I'm famished!' she exclaimed with an overly dramatic sigh, in an attempt to break the tense atmosphere with a change of topic. 'Can I suggest we break for lunch before we start on your mum's personal life? Because I have a feeling...' she looked at him with a grimace '...that we may need some fortification to get through it. And my body armour is back in London.'

'Famished?' Mark replied, blinking for a few seconds as though his brain was trying to process the words. Then his shoulders seemed to drop several inches, his back straightened and his head lifted. 'Of course. In that case it's my turn to provide lunch. Prepare to have your taste buds tantalised by one of the excellent tavernas on the coast. How does a big bowl of crisp Greek salad followed by succulent freshly caught sea bass and chips sound? But there's one condition. We don't talk about our jobs or why you're here. Do we have a deal?'

Lexi's mouth watered at the thought of it. Her last proper meal had been in Hong Kong two days earlier. Although lunch for two in a beautiful restaurant by the ocean could be mighty distracting if it meant sitting across the table from Mark for several hours, sharing delicious food.

'Lunch in a restaurant?' She baulked. 'Do we have the time?' She thought in panic of the mountain of paperwork they'd just left behind. 'There's a lot of work to do here.'

'Which is why the fresh sea air will do both of us a

world of good. I've been cooped up inside for the last three days. I need a break and a change of scene.'

'Why don't you go on your own?' She smiled, nodding her head. 'It'll take me a few hours to read through these typed pages in detail. I'll be quite happy with bread and salad.'

'You can do that later,' he shot back and looked at her through narrowed eyes. 'Unless, of course, there's another reason why you'd prefer not to eat lunch in public with me. Jealous boyfriend? Secret fiancé? Or simply worried about my table manners?'

He tilted his head and the tingles hit her the second those blue eyes twinkled in her direction.

'Just say the word and I can provide excellent references for both my sobriety and my familiarity with cutlery.'

Lexi rolled her eyes. Mark was clearly determined to avoid what they had left behind in that suitcase of memories, so she relented enough to step back from the balustrade and shake her head.

'No jealous boyfriends—or girlfriends, for that matter— no secret fiancé, and I'm confident that your table manners will be excellent. Okay, we have a deal.' Her face softened. 'However, there is one tiny problem.'

His eyebrows lifted.

'Oh, yes, I know it's hard to believe. I hate to admit this, but I didn't have the heart to move the kittens out of the car last night. Can we walk there? Catch the bus?'

Mark pushed his right hand into his pocket and took a step closer, filling the air between them with a few inches of warm masculine scent. He pulled out a set of keys and swung them into his left hand. 'No problem. I'm ready to go. How about you?'

'You mean now? I need a few minutes to get changed and grab a bag,' Lexi replied and twirled her forefinger towards her head. 'And do my hair and put some make-up on.'

He looked at her open-mouthed for a few seconds, and then did a complete head-to-toe scan of every item of cloth-ing that she was wearing. And actually smiled as he was doing it.

Lexi crossed her arms and glared at him. She felt as though his X-ray vision actually bored right through her trousers and the off-the-shoulder tunic to the brand-new red-lace lingerie beneath. Her neck was burning with em-barrassment, her palms were sweating, and the longer he looked the more heated she became. This was not doing much good for her composure.

'Oh, I really wouldn't worry about that,' he murmured. 'Especially about your hair.'

'What's wrong with my hair?' Lexi asked, flicking her hair out from inside her collar and away from the back of her neck. 'Is there a dress code where we're going?'

A peal of pure exuberant laughter came out of Mark's mouth and echoed around the garden. The sound was so astonishing, so warm and natural, that Lexi blinked twice to make sure she was looking at the same person. *Where had that come from?*

And could she please hear it again? Because his whole face had been transformed into a smiling, almost *happy* version of the usual handsome-but-stern exterior. And her poor foolish heart jumped up and did a merry jig just from looking at him.

She'd thought Mark handsome before, but this was tak-ing it to a new level.

'You'll be fine,' Mark replied, looking rather sheepish at his outburst of jollity. And then he held out his hand to-wards her, as though he was daring her to come with him.

'I'm going to need five minutes,' she said, trying to

sound bright and enthusiastic as she slid past him and tried to ignore his hand. 'Just enough time for you to bring the car around.'

'You don't need five minutes,' he replied with a grin, grabbing her hand and half dragging her off the patio and onto the gravel drive. 'And who said anything about a car?'

'Your carriage awaits, madam.'

Lexi stared at the motorcycle, then at the boyish black crash helmet Mark was holding, then back to the motorcycle. She stepped out onto the gravel and walked slowly around the vehicle, examining it from a number of angles.

Mark waited patiently for a few seconds as Lexi stopped and nodded her head several times, before declaring, 'This is a scooter.'

'Your powers of observation are quite superlative,' he replied, fighting the urge to smile and thereby shatter even more of her expectations.

'It's a very nice scooter,' she continued, 'and very clean for a boy, but…it's still a scooter.'

She seemed to suck in a breath, then shook her head twice and looked up at him with total bewilderment on her face.

'But *you* can't ride a scooter! It must be against the rules for English aristocrats to ride scooters. At the very least I expected some swanky sports car worth more than my house. This is incredibly shocking.'

'I take delight in thwarting your expectations. For where we're going, two-wheeled transport is definitely the best option.'

And with that he calmly unfastened a second crash helmet from the back seat and presented her with it. The helmet was red, with a white lightning arrow down each side and the words *Paxos Pizza* in large black letters across the front. Not something you could easily miss.

'Ah. Yes. Cassie's helmet came at a bargain price. That was the only one my pal Spiro had left in a medium.'

She looked dubiously at the helmet that he was holding out to her.

'The only one? I see. And you're quite positive that we shouldn't take my hire car?'

'Quite,' he replied. 'I would hate to disturb the cats.'

'Ah,' she said, 'of course. The cats. A man clearly has to have priorities.'

Without saying another word she slid her shoulder bag over her head and across her chest, took the helmet out of his hands, swept back her hair and slipped the helmet on. All in one single sleek movement. She fastened the chinstrap as though she had been doing it all her life.

His silent admiration just clicked up two points.

'Don't say a word,' she murmured, glaring at him through slitted eyes.

'I wouldn't dare.' Mark patted the seat behind him. 'You might want to hold on to me when we set off.'

'Oh, I think I can manage. Thank you all the same.'

She was standing next to him now, one hand planted firmly on each hip, weighing up her options. Although she was only two feet away, he could hear her mind ticking. The air crackled with tension.

'You should be warm enough,' he said quite calmly. 'We're not going far.'

And with that he started the engine and clicked down into first gear.

Then he checked the chinstrap on his helmet, wriggled his bottom into the driver's position and faced directly ahead. Without looking back even once to check what she was doing.

Ten seconds later the bike lurched slightly to one side as she settled herself on the small pillion passenger seat.

That was his cue to enjoy a totally secret wide-mouthed smile, which he knew she wouldn't see.

'Hang on!' he called, and without waiting for a reply opened up the throttle and set off slowly down the drive. He checked the road was clear and they were on their way.

Warm summer air, thick with pollen from the olive trees and scented with pine resin, caressed Lexi's arms and bare legs as the scooter tootled down the main road heading for the coast.

She leaned back on her arms and gripped on to the grab-rail behind her seat, her muscles clenching and rattling with every bump in the road. Strange how she hadn't noticed the potholes in the comfort of her hire car. She was certainly feeling every one of them now.

She hated being a passenger. But she had to admit that the view in front of her was impressive enough. Mark's broad shoulders filled his shirt, and as he stretched forward on the scooter she could see the muscles in his arms move effortlessly through the controls. His top wasn't quite long enough, which meant she had occasional tantalising glimpses of the band of skin above his snug-fitting trousers.

Far too tantalising.

Dratted tingles.

Lexi turned her head slowly from side to side, looking for distraction in the stunning Greek countryside as they sped along at about twenty miles an hour. Lemon trees, bright purple and pink bougainvillaea, and pale oleander bushes filled the gardens of the houses they passed on the small country road. Dark green cypresses and pine trees

created a perfect skyline of light and shade under the deep
azure blue of the sky.

And all the time she could glimpse a narrow line of
darker blue in between the trees, where the Ionian Sea
met the horizon.

The sun shone warmly on her exposed skin and she
felt free and wild and ready to explore. She felt so completely liberated that, without thinking about it, she closed
her eyes and relaxed back to let the wind cool her throat
and neck. Just as she did so the bike slowed, making a
sharp turn to the left off the main road onto what felt like
a farm track.

Lexi snapped her eyes open and instinctively grabbed
Mark around the waist, her heart thumping. She could feel
his muscles tighten under her hands, warm and solid and
mightily reassuring.

He glanced back just once, to give her a reassuring
smile, before reducing his speed and leaning the scooter
through bend after bend of steadily narrowing and even
more bumpy road until they came to a passing point outside a stunning tiny white church and he came to a slow,
graceful stop.

They had arrived. At the end of the road.

'Did I mention that the rest of the way is on foot?' he
asked in an innocent voice.

Lexi replied with a scathing look and glanced down
at her gold wedge sandals. 'How far do I have to walk?'

'Five minutes. Tops. It's just at the end of the donkey
trail and then through the olives.'

'Five minutes? I'll hold you to that. Of course you *do*
realise that your terrible secret is now out in the open?'
Lexi grinned, heading down the rocky path between the
high drystone walls that separated the olive groves. Pine
needles from the conifers softened her tread.

Mark swallowed hard. 'Any one in particular? I have so many.'

'This is undoubtedly true. I was, of course, referring to the secret life of The Honourable Mark Belmont, Company Director. The outside world knows him as the suave financial wizard of the London stock market. But when Mr Belmont comes to Paxos? Ah, then the other Mark emerges from his chrysalis. *This* version enjoys riding his scooter—in public—drinking the local wine and entertaining cats. So that only leaves one question. What other hidden talents are yet to emerge?'

His reply was a quick snort.

'Landscape painting, perhaps? No. Too sedate. How about speedboat-racing?' Lexi stretched up and ran her fingers through the low-hanging branch of an olive tree. 'Or perhaps you're the olive king of the island and have vats of the stuff back at Belmont Manor, ready to challenge the Greek olive-oil market? That'd suit your aristocratic swashbuckling style.'

He chuckled out loud now. A real laugh, displaying his perfect teeth. 'Swashbuckling? Not exactly my style. And, in answer to your question, I'm no water baby. But I can heartily recommend the local olive oil.'

'You don't swashbuckle *or* swim?'

'Never.'

'Seriously? When you have that lovely pool at the villa?'

He froze, half turned and then looked at her for a split second, still smiling. 'Swimming was for pupils who preferred sport to studying. Apart from my stellar football experience, which was definitely a one-off, sport was not on my timetable. And it strikes me that I've been answering a lot of questions. Your turn. What hidden talents does Lexi Sloane have up her sleeve? What's *her* guilty pleasure?'

Now it was Lexi's turn to smile, but she shot him a quick glance as they walked along before speaking again.

'Apart from good food and wine, you mean? Ah. Well, as a matter of fact I *do* have a guilty pleasure. I write children's stories.'

Mark made a strange strangled sound but carried on walking.

'Children's stories? You mean teen vampire love and schools for wizards?'

She sniggered. 'Mine are meant for a much younger audience. Think talking animals and fairies.' She stopped walking, dived into her shoulder bag, brought out her favourite notebook and flicked to a particular page. 'I worked on this one during the night when I couldn't sleep.'

Mark turned around on the narrow path and took a step towards her, peering at the notebook she held out.

To Lexi's delight his eyes widened and a broad grin warmed his face, as though she'd lit a fire inside him which drove away the darkness of the morning with its brightness.

'That's Snowy One and Snowy Two.' He laughed, flicking over the page. 'These are wonderful! You didn't mention that you did the illustrations, as well. When did you find the time to draw the kittens?'

'I cheated and took some photos before dinner yesterday. They were perfect models and quite happy to stay in position for at least a couple of seconds while I found a pose I liked. Then I worked the photos into the stories.'

She took the notebook back and just for a fraction of a second her fingertips made contact with Mark's hand. And, judging by his sharp intake of breath, he felt the connection just as powerfully as she did. He immediately started gabbling to cover it up.

'Well, I am impressed. Are you planning to have your

stories published or keep them for your own children to enjoy?'

And there it was. A direct hit. Bullseye. Right between the eyes!

My own children? Oh, Mark, if only you knew how much I long to have children of my own.

Tears pricked at the corners of her eyes. *Stupid.* She should be able to handle the question better than this. But he'd hit her with it out of the blue. That was all. She could cope.

'Published, I hope,' she replied through a burning throat. 'One day.'

'Excellent,' he replied, his warm voice brimming with feeling. 'In that case I look forward to reading your stories to my nephews at the earliest opportunity.'

Lexi picked up his lighter mood and went with it gladly. 'Ah. Do I have to add bedtime story-reader to your long list of accomplishments?'

He smiled. 'I try. Actually...' He paused long enough for Lexi to look at him, then shrugged. 'Sometimes reading those stories is the best part of my day. We have a great time.'

With startling suddenness he turned away from her and started down the track, but the sadness and need in his voice were so powerful that Lexi stayed frozen to the spot.

Two things were clear. He loved those boys. And Mark Belmont was going to be a wonderful father to the lucky children he so clearly wanted in his life.

And her poor heart cried at the thought that she would probably never experience that joy.

Just as the thought popped into her head Mark glanced back towards her, and Lexi slid the book back into her bag and pretended to rummage around as she casually replied, 'I don't have any food with me except breath mints.'

Then she looked around her and raised her eyebrows. 'And, while I appreciate that this is a lovely spot, and I'm enjoying the countryside, something tells me that there won't be a restaurant at the end of this very winding footpath. Am I right?'

'Perhaps.'

'Sorry?'

'It's a long story.'

He gestured with his hand down the path and set off slowly. 'You were talking earlier about collecting impressions about a person by where they liked to live and what they read. And it struck me that you might find it easier to understand who Crystal Leighton was when she wasn't being a famous actress if I showed you her favourite place on the island. I haven't been here in a long time, but this is very special. If we're lucky it won't have changed that much.'

'What kind of place are you talking about?' Lexi asked, astonished that Crystal had chosen somewhere other than her lovely villa. 'And what makes it so special?'

'Come and see for yourself,' Mark replied in a hushed voice that she had never heard him use before.

Lexi followed him through a cluster of pine trees, pushed through some fragrant flowering bushes next to a stone wall, and stepped into a private garden.

And what she saw there was so astonishing that she had to clutch on to Mark for support. His reaction was to instantly wrap one long muscular arm around her waist to hold her safe against his body.

They were standing about six feet from the edge of a cliff. A real cliff. As in the type of cliff where, if you stepped forward one inch, you'd find yourself flying through space for a long time before hitting the sea below.

Their only protection from the dizzyingly close edge

was a waist-high stone wall, which had been built in a wide curve in front of a low stone bench.

But it was the view that grabbed her and held her even tighter than Mark. All she could see in each direction was an unbroken band of sea and the azure sky above it. She felt like an explorer standing on the edge of a new world, looking out over an ocean no one had ever seen before, with nothing but air between her and the sea and the sky. And all she had to do was reach out and it would be hers.

To her right and left were high white cliffs of solid rock, studded with occasional stunted pine trees like the ones she was standing next to now. Far below, the sea crashed onto a collection of huge boulders at the foot of the cliffs.

'There are huge caves under the cliff here,' Mark said as though he was reading her thoughts. 'Big enough for the tourist boats to go into. But we're quite safe. There are hundreds of feet of solid rock below us.' As if to prove the point he grabbed her hand and practically dragged her to the stone wall, so that they could look out together over the tops of the hardy bushes and bright flowering plants clinging to the cliff face at the open sea.

'This is the nearest I've ever come to being on the prow of a ship,' Lexi breathed. 'Oh, Mark. This is…wonderful. I can see now why she chose this spot.'

'You should come back at dusk and watch the sun set-ting. It turns the whole sky a burning red. It's a wonderful sight. And, best of all, it's totally private. No cameras, no people, just you and the sea and the sky. That was why she loved it so much here. That's why she spent hour after hour on her own up here with just a picnic and a book. Alone with her thoughts. Away from the press and the movie business and everything that came with it.'

Lexi glanced up at Mark's face but his attention was totally fixed on the horizon, where the sky met the sea.

His eyes were the colour of the ocean. His fingers were still locked on to hers and she could feel his heart pound with each breath.

And her heart melted like cheese under a grill.

She had not intended it to. *Far from it.*

She couldn't help it. The fire in his voice and in his heart burned too hot to resist.

Which was why she did something very foolish. She squeezed his hand.

Instantly he glanced down at his fingers, and she caught a glimpse of awareness and recognition that he had revealed a little too much of himself before he recovered and released her with a brief twist of his mouth.

'Last Christmas she tried to persuade me to take some time off to celebrate Easter with her on the island. Just the two of us. But I said no. Too much work.' He sniffed, looking out towards the islands in the distance. 'Ironic, isn't it? I have the time now.'

'She knew you wanted to come back. I'm sure of it. How could you not? When you write about the last few months of her life you should put that in. It would be a lovely touch to end her story.'

She instantly sensed his solid-steel defences moving back into place.

'I'm not ready to write about how her life ended. I'm not sure I ever will be.'

'But you have to, Mark,' Lexi urged him softly, ignoring just how close the cliff edge was so she could step in front of him, forcing him to look down at her face. 'You're the only one who can tell the truth about what happened that day. Because if you don't someone else will make it up. I know that for a fact. Your mother is relying on you. Don't you want the truth to come out?'

'The truth? Oh, Lexi.'

She lifted her hands and pressed her fingertips to the front of his shirt.

He flinched at her touch, but she didn't move an inch and locked her eyes on to his.

'I was only there for a few seconds that day, but you saw what happened in its entirety, and you know why it happened. That makes you unique.'

'What happened?' he repeated, his eyes scanning her face as though he was looking for permission to say what needed to be said and finding it. 'What happened was that I was half a world away from London when my mother collapsed with a brain aneurysm. Dad had sent me over to Mumbai to negotiate with the owners of a start-up technology firm, so I was in India when Mum's friend called me out of the blue. It was the middle of the night, but there's nothing like hearing that your mother's been rushed to hospital to wake you up pretty fast.'

'How awful. No one should have to take a call like that when they're so far away.'

'The next twenty-four hours were probably the longest and most exhausting of my life. But if anything it got worse when I finally arrived. Cassie had met me at the airport. I'll never forget walking into that hospital room. I hardly recognised her. She had tubes coming out from everywhere, she was surrounded by medical staff, and I couldn't understand why she was still comatose. She looked so lifeless, so white and still.'

He shook his head and closed his eyes as Lexi moved closer towards him.

'I think I must have been too exhausted at that point to take things in, because I remember asking Cassie if she was sure there hadn't been some terrible mistake—this wasn't our mother after all. But then the doctors whisked us all out to one of those beige and green so-called relatives' rooms and the truth finally started to hit home.'

He half opened his eyes as Lexi looked into his face. 'Our lovely, beautiful mother hadn't come to London to stay with her old friend and talk charity fundraising. She'd come to have plastic surgery. She didn't tell us in advance because she knew we'd try and talk her out of it. According to her friend, she'd planned the surgery months earlier, as a Christmas present to herself. Because she needed the boost to her confidence.'

'Oh, Mark.'

'She had the operation Monday morning, collapsed on the Monday evening, and slipped away from us on Thursday morning. While I was standing in a police station in central London, being cautioned for attacking a member of the press. Your father.'

Mark snapped his fingers, and the sound ricocheted out into the serene calm air and seemed to penetrate Lexi's body. She jerked back in shock.

'*That's* how fast your life can switch.'

Lexi felt tears roll down her cheeks, but she couldn't speak. Not yet. Not until he was ready.

'The surgeon kept telling us that if she'd survived the aneurysm she could well have been brain-damaged or disabled, as if that would help in some way. It didn't.'

'How did your dad get through it?' Lexi asked.

'He didn't,' Mark whispered. 'He fought off cancer a few years ago, and was in remission until her death destroyed him. He's never been the same since. It's as though all the light went out of his world. He's fighting it, but he's determined to do it alone and there's not one thing Cassie or I can do except make his days as bright and positive as possible.'

'And do you think this book will help? Is that why you agreed to do it?'

'Cassie thinks it's the one thing keeping his spirits up. He wants it to be a celebration of her life instead of some nonsense tabloid journalists will put together from media press kits to make a profit from some scandalous headline.'

'But what about you, Mark? What would help *you* to grieve for her?'

'Me? I don't know where to start. Sometimes I can't believe that I won't ever see her again or hear her voice. I don't want to think about all the future events and special occasions in my life where there will be an empty chair with her name on it. And then there's the guilt. That's the toughest thing of all.'

'Guilt? Why do you feel guilty?'

He closed his eyes. 'Let me see. Never having time to spend with my own mother one-to-one because of the obligations I took on when Edmund died. Always cancelling lunch dates with my biggest fan at the very last minute or having to cut short telephone calls because of some business meeting. Oh, yes, and let's not forget the big one. The reason she had plastic surgery in the first place.'

Mark lifted his head and looked directly at Lexi. She could see moisture glistening at the corners of his eyes, but was powerless to speak in the intensity of his gaze.

'She told her friend that she was having the surgery because she didn't want to let me down at my engagement party. She didn't feel beautiful enough to stand next to me and my future bride's aristocratic family. So she went to London on her own and went through surgery on her own. *For me.* Have you ever heard anything so ridiculous in your life?'

CHAPTER SEVEN

'OH MARK,' Lexi whispered in amazement. 'Why do you think your mother felt that way? She was stunningly beautiful.'

Mark looked up as a flock of seabirds circled above their heads before flying over to the cliffs to nest. 'Pressure. Competition from other actresses for work in TV and movies. Every time we met she talked about the disappointment of being turned down for the roles she really wanted to play.' Mark sighed. 'She couldn't get work, and it was obvious she was finding it tougher and tougher to bounce back from each new rejection. Her agent gave up even trying to interest the movie studios. There was always another beautiful starlet just waiting to be discovered, and in the end it wore her down.'

'But Crystal Leighton was still a big star. People loved her.'

'Try telling that to the casting directors. The truth is she'd been desperately unhappy for a very long time and it showed. She'd lost her spark. Her vitality. Her joy. And it was there on her face for the world to see.'

'So it wasn't just about your engagement party, was it? That was just an excuse for having the work done. Please don't feel guilty about something you have no control over.

From what you tell me, it doesn't sound like you would've been able to change her mind.'

Mark exhaled slowly and Lexi felt his breath on her face. She lifted her right hand and stroked his cheek with her fingertips as his eyes fluttered half-closed. 'I didn't realise you were engaged,' she whispered, desperate to prolong the sensation of standing so close to him for as long as possible. Even if there *was* a fabulous fiancée waiting for him back in London.

'There's no reason why you should. It never happened. It's over now,' Mark replied, his brow furrowed and hard. 'We'd known each other for years, we mixed in the same circles, and I think it just became something other people expected us to do. I never proposed and she didn't expect me to. It was simply a convenient arrangement for both of us. We were friends, but I wasn't in love with her. Two months ago she found someone she truly cares about, which is how it should be.'

'Did your mother know you felt that way?'

'I don't know. We never talked about it. We don't talk about things in our family. We skate over the surface for fear of falling into the deep icy water below. And all my father cared about was making sure there'd be another Belmont son to inherit the title.'

Mark shook his head, his mouth a firm narrow line. 'I thought for a while that I wanted the same thing. That perhaps having a wife and a family might bring the Belmont family back together again. But it would only have made two more people miserable and led to an embarrassing divorce down the line. I can see that now.'

Lexi's brain caught up with what Mark was saying and a cold hand gripped her heart in spite of the warm breeze. 'You were prepared to do that?' she asked, trying to keep the horror of his situation out of her voice and failing. 'To marry a girl whom you didn't love? Then have a baby with her to provide a son to inherit the estate?'

'Oh, yes. The old rules are still in force. Even Cassie's boys don't stand a chance. Unless I persuade some poor girl to give me a son, the next Baron Belmont will be my least favourite cousin. And both of *his* boys are adopted, so they can't inherit, either. So that's it. Nine hundred years, father to son, and it all comes down to me.'

Lexi sucked in a breath and exhaled slowly. 'How can you stand it? How can you live like that?' she asked in a trembling voice. 'Bringing a child into this world should be something for two people to celebrate—not an obligation you can tick off the list.'

And at least you're able to have a son. Have you no idea how lucky you are?

Then she looked into Mark's sad eyes and all of her fight drifted away. 'Sorry. That was unfair. You have a duty to your family and they need you.'

His response was to rest his forehead against Lexi's and take her hand in his, stretching out each of her fingers in turn, as though they were the most fascinating objects he'd ever seen.

'Now do you understand why I'm struggling to finish her biography?' he asked, his voice low and trembling. 'People will expect my mother to have enjoyed a fabulous life full of fun and happiness and excitement. Movie stars like Crystal Leighton aren't supposed to end up living a bitter, cold existence, racked with disappointment and low self-worth. With a son who was never there for her.'

He clasped both her hands between his and held them prisoner before asking the question Lexi had been dreading but had somehow known would come.

'How will you write *that* story, Lexi? How do you tell

that kind of truth without destroying my father and my family at the same time?'

'That has to be your decision, Mark,' she replied, in as low and calm a voice as she could manage. 'I can tell you how to make this book a true celebration of her life. And I know that the dark and the shade only make the happy times seem brighter. That was a part of her life and you can't avoid the truth.'

'The truth? That's a strange concept from someone who writes stories for a living. Let me tell *you* the truth,' he murmured, his voice trembling with emotion. 'The truth is that I need to get back to London. Away from the manor. I have to focus on the future and learn to live my own life, not a second-hand one—that's precisely what she would want me to do.'

And then Mark released her fingers, pressed one hand to her cheek, tilted his head and, with the most feather-light touch, kissed her.

Lexi was so startled that she was rendered speechless. The pressure of his lips was so warm and soft that her eyelids fluttered closed and she almost leant forward for more—only to find him gone. And she immediately cursed herself for being so weak and foolish.

'Thank you for listening. I can't finish this book, Lexi. I can't put my family through the pain.' He took a step back and looked out over the cliffs to the wide blue ocean in front of them. 'Sorry, Lexi. The biography is cancelled. I'm going to return the advance to my publisher. I can deal with the fallout with my family, and it's better to do it now rather than later, in the full face of the media. Thank you for helping me to decide to move forward in my life, not backwards, but I don't need your help any more. You can go back to London. Your work here is finished.'

* * *

Lexi fought to bring her heartbeat back to normal before stomping up to Mark, who was standing at the stone wall looking out towards the islands on the horizon.

'Finished? Oh, no, you don't, Mark Belmont.'

Mark turned back to face her, startled. 'I beg your pardon?'

'And so you should. Because right now it seems to me that you are running away from a challenge just at the point when it starts to get interesting.'

He smiled and shook his head. 'I've already told you that you will get your fee. Don't worry about it.'

She stepped forward, grabbed his arms and turned him sideways, so that he was not quite so scarily close to the edge of the precipice.

'I'm really not getting through to you, am I?' She rolled her eyes. 'I refuse to let you walk away from the only chance you'll ever have to put the record straight about Crystal Leighton. Yes, that's right. I am not going anywhere. And neither are you. I've been hearing a lot about family obligations, but nothing about how the real Mark would choose to celebrate his mother's life and work if left to himself.'

'That option is not available. I don't have a choice.'

Lexi clamped her hands over her ears. 'Not listening. Of course you have choices. You're the one who decides what to do with the life you've been given. So you're going to be the next Baron Belmont? That's amazing!'

She lowered her hands and smiled at him. 'Think of all the good you can do in your position. Starting with celebrating the life of your wonderful mother.'

One more step pressed her against his chest. 'Take the risk, Mark. Take this week out of your life and do the best you can. Because together I know we can create something stunning and true and authentic. But I need you on my team. Come on. Take the risk. You know you'll always regret it if you don't. And I never took you for a quitter.' Her voice softened. 'Do it out of love, not out of obligation. Who knows? You might actually enjoy it.'

His finger traced a line from her cheek to her neck and the tingles made her want to squirm.

'One week?' he whispered, his breath hot on her face.

'One week.' She play-thumped him on the chest. 'Now. Where's that lunch you promised me? I've been desperate for Greek salad for the last hour.'

It was a very silly hour of the morning when Lexi finally gave up tossing and turning, pulled her pillow from under her head and attempted to throw back the covers from her comfortable double bed.

Only she'd twisted so much that the fine cotton sheets had wrapped around her like an Egyptian mummy, and after a few minutes of kicking and elbowing her way free she knew what silkworms must feel like. She felt so hot that even the single sheet was a weight on her skin. The simple air-conditioning unit was trying its best, but with the double glazed windows closed the bedroom felt airless and stuffy. And so desperately, desperately quiet.

Somewhere in the house a clock was striking every quarter-hour with a musical chime, but apart from that comforting sound the house was completely silent—as though it was a sleeping giant waiting for some magical spell to be broken to bring him back to life.

It was such a total contrast to the background hubbub of the large international hotels she usually stayed in and the city noises that surrounded them.

Lexi tiptoed over to the balcony door and peeked out through the hand-worked lace curtain. Slowly and quietly sneaking open the door, she stepped outside, closing it behind her.

She could see light coming from the living rooms of the house on the other side of the olive grove. Moths fluttered against the light above her head, but no mosquitoes, thank goodness. Down below in the garden, solar-powered lights illuminated the pathway to the pool and a barbecue area. A white cat pattered across the patio tiles towards the swimming pool—probably the Snowys' dad Oscar, going for a drink. But apart from that all was still, calm and serene.

Lexi looked out over the treetops and soaked in the silence as though she was drinking the contents of a deep well of cool, refreshing water. True silence like this was so rare in her life that when it happened she took the time to appreciate the tranquillity, no matter how temporary it might be.

Especially after today's scooter ride to the viewpoint.

It was going to take a while to process everything that Mark had told her. And what about that fleeting kiss? Oh, boy. Had he really no clue as to how totally tantalising it was to have had a taste of his mouth, so tender, even for such a fleeting second?

He'd made an effort to keep their conversation on neutral ground during their brief lunch at the lovely harbour at Lakka before going straight back to work. And this time they had both been enthusiastic and motivated. The tide had turned. Now Mark wanted this book as much as she did.

Perhaps it was this villa that had made the difference.

Everything seemed so still. So full of possibility. A white clean space just begging to be filled with activity and life and—

A loud clattering, quickly followed by a low mumble, banged out on the wooden floorboards and she practically jumped over the railing. The sound ricocheted like a bullet around the terrace, shattering the deep silence.

Holding her breath, she clung on to the railing and listened for any further indication of movement. Or for the sound of his voice.

He did have a remarkable voice—deep and intense, yet quiet. With that faint touch of an American accent. It truly was quite delicious.

She wondered for a moment what it would be like to hear that voice speaking her name with intimate, loving tenderness. To fall into those strong arms and not let go for any reason.

No! Wipe that image from your brain!

If she wanted a fantasy she would stick to thinking about her mother's engagement party and all the work they needed to do to make it as magical as possible.

So what if she was attracted to him? It was only natural. But there could never be anything between them. And she had better remember that.

Lexi took another step along the small balcony, gazing out over the olive groves towards the sea.

A ship was sailing on the horizon, the rows of coloured lights on its decks bright and sharp against the darkness of the night. Perhaps it was a cruise ship, or a large ferry from Italy. And above the ship the sky was a breathtaking blanket of stars. She leant on the balustrade and stood on the tips of her toes, but the overhanging wooden eaves were blocking her view.

There was only one thing for it: she would have to go outside to get the full benefit of the night sky.

Lexi skipped lightly down the staircase, carefully turned the creaking handle of the heavy door that opened onto the patio, anxious not to disturb Mark, and stepped out onto the stone floor.

She stood silently with her head back for a second, lost in the bliss of cool air against her skin. A gentle breeze was blowing in from the sea between the pine trees, and Lexi could smell flowers and pine resin mixed in with the slight whiff of chlorine from the swimming pool.

A tiny sliver of new moon peeked out from behind one of the cypresses across the lane, and the only light was from the solar-powered lamps around the car park and stone steps leading to the house. But as she made her way gingerly towards the side garden in her bare feet even that background light was blocked by the house.

Perfect! Lexi stopped, pressed her back against the wall, and looked up towards the night sky.

Without streetlights or a city glow, the sky was wonderfully dark and clear of cloud. Spread out above the trees was a magnificent display of stars which seemed dazzlingly bright in the unpolluted air. She even recognised a few of the constellations, although they were aligned in slightly different shapes from the ones she knew in England.

It was stunning. Without realising it Lexi exhaled a long, slow sigh of deep satisfaction and relaxation. Her shoulders slumped with pleasure.

'Stargazing? Can't blame you. It is rather spectacular.'

She practically jumped out of her skin.

There was a creak from the sun lounger at the far end of the patio, and as Lexi's eyes became more accustomed to the low light she saw Mark stretched out flat, hands behind his head. He seemed to be fully dressed, and she could only hope that her thin pyjamas were not too transparent.

'Well!' She tried to keep her voice light, jovial and her heart from exploding. 'This is a surprise. The famous businessman Mark Belmont is actually a closet astronomer. One more attribute to add to your résumé.'

He chuckled, and his voice was low, deep and resonant in the absolute stillness of the night.

'Guilty as charged,' he replied. 'Always have been. Even had a telescope at one time—much to my family's amusement. My sister could probably find it somewhere in the attic if needed. How about you? Long history of solar exploration in your family?'

'Oh, just one of my many talents,' Lexi replied and was just about to make some dismissive quip when it struck her that from the tone of his voice he sounded relaxed and comfortable. At home. Unencumbered with responsibility.

So she fought back the urge to be sarcastic and strolled over towards his lounger in the dark. Except that her bare toes connected with something solid on the way.

'Ouch!' She winced. 'What have I just banged into?'

'That would be the other lounger,' he replied, sounding concerned. 'Any damage done?'

'To my toe or your furniture?' she asked and flexed her toes. 'No, I don't think so. I still have some movement. I can't speak for the other party.'

'Excellent,' he replied. 'Then please feel free to sprawl and enjoy the free floorshow. No charge.'

'Well, in that case, I think I might just do that.' Lexi smiled as she sank her bottom into the sumptuous cushion and stretched her legs out. 'Oh, that's better.'

They lay there without speaking for a few minutes, disturbed only by the sound of the cicadas in the olive groves and the occasional car horn from miles away. It was so bizarrely quiet that when a weird whooping, screeching noise broke the silence Lexi sat bolt upright and clutched the sun lounger in alarm.

'What was that?' she whispered.

'An owl. They nest in the trees,' Mark replied. 'So, tell me more about your star-watching.'

Lexi knew from the warmth of his voice that he was smiling as he said it. 'I can't say it was a popular hobby in my family, but I've always been fascinated by the stars.' She snuggled deeper into the lounger and tried to find a comfier position. 'I can still remember the first time one of the teachers at school told us that each star was actually a sun and probably had a moon and planets going around it.'

Lexi chuckled. 'He had no idea what he'd started. I dragged my poor mother out on cold winter nights, huddled up outside the back door of our little London house, just to stare up at the sky. I remember asking her if there were people like us living on those planets around those stars, looking back at us at that very minute.'

'What was her reply?' Mark murmured in the dark.

'She said there probably were creatures and possibly even intelligent beings living on those planets, orbiting around suns we can't even see because they're so far away that the light hasn't reached us yet from those distant worlds.' She paused for a second. 'Which totally made my head spin. Clever woman, my mother.'

Except when it came to choosing husbands. Then she was a disaster.

'Do you still live with her? In your little house in London?'

'Mum? No. I moved out earlier this year—although we still live in the same part of London. I spend a lot of time overseas, but we make the time to catch up with each other every few months. Our telephone bills are pretty enormous. It works well. She recently got engaged, so the next few months are going to be a bit wedding-crazy.'

Lexi pursed her lips for a second. The conversation was starting to get a little personal, and way too close to home for this audience. Especially when it came to her parents.

'How about you, Mark? Tell me about your place in London.'

'I have the penthouse apartment in my office building.'

'You live in your office building?' she replied, realising even as she spoke that her voice was stinging with criticism.

A low snort came from the other lounger, but when he spoke Mark's voice was clear and honest, rather than embarrassed or apologetic for living above the shop. 'It suits me very well. I'm single and busy. And the views across the city are pretty spectacular from my balcony. But the stars? Ah. Not so spectacular.'

Lexi exhaled slowly. 'It must be wonderful to have this house to come back to any time you want and look at the night sky. You do know that this is every writer's dream? A quiet rural retreat where they can focus on simply being creative. It's magical.'

The silence seemed even more intense and Lexi squeezed her eyes closed. Why had she said that? *Stupid girl.* He might think she was angling for an invitation. Or more.

'That's the problem,' he replied in a very quiet voice. 'It is magical, but most of the year the place stays empty and the only people who benefit are the cats and my housekeeper. We're always so very, very busy. Always so much to do just to stand still.'

The sadness in his voice pierced Lexi's gentle heart.

She hadn't expected to like him or care about him, but she did. More than was good for her. She knew now that his family life wasn't perfect and happy after all, and she was sorry for that. So much loss and pain changed people, and not always for the better. But Mark? Mark still had that spark, even if it was hidden deep inside.

And the thought that he might lose that spark sent a shiver down her back. She quivered and rubbed her arms.

'Feeling cold?' he asked.

'A little,' she replied. 'Probably time for me to head back inside.'

She heard a low grunt and a shuffle as Mark swung himself off his lounger and took the two steps towards her. Before she had a chance to speak he had taken both her hands in his and was lifting her to her feet.

'We stargazers have to stick together,' he murmured, pressing his body against the length of her back with his arms around her waist. A delicious glow of warmth and strength filled Lexi's body and she instinctively leant back to enjoy the heat from his closeness.

Mark raised one arm and pointed to a bright star on the horizon below the new moon. 'I used to read all those exciting comics about mysterious invaders from Venus or Mars. Scared myself silly. I suspect that's why my dad bought me the telescope. So that hard science could replace dreams and fantasy stories about aliens and spaceships.'

'And what about your mum? What did she say?' Lexi struggled to keep her voice steady in the face of this sudden intimacy.

'Oh, she kept bringing me the comics. Keeping my mind open to every option. I loved her for that.'

'She must have been quite remarkable,' Lexi whispered into the night.

'Yes. Yes, she was.' He paused before going on. 'Thanks for talking me into carrying on with her biography. I think it's going to be a grand celebration.'

Lexi lowered her head and turned around so that she was facing Mark.

'You're most welcome. Good night. I hope you sleep well.'

She touched her cool fingers to either side of his face, and brushed her lips against his in a light kiss which was just a tiny bit longer than the one he had given her at the viewpoint. His lips were warm and full and inviting, and she hesitated for just a moment in the darkness before moving away.

Mark seemed to freeze. Then he took hold of her shoulders, pulled her tight into his body, stepped forward until her back was resting against the wall of the house, cushioned by his arm, so that when he kissed her, her pliant body had somewhere to go.

This was nothing like that first hesitant kiss in the sunshine. This was the kiss of a man determined to drive logical thought from her mind as he pressed harder, exploring her tongue and lips while taking the weight of her body in his muscular arms.

Her hands moved up from his shoulders and into his hair, which was as wonderful and sensual as she had imagined.

But she had broken the spell by moving. And he eased back, drawing her on wobbly legs away from the wall.

She hung on to him, her head against his chest until her breathing calmed, then looked up into his smiling face. His thumb brushed against her lower lip, sending tingles to places she really did not want to be tingling.

'You are really quite irresistible. Do you know that?' he whispered.

She managed a nod. 'You, too.'

He stifled a grin. 'But probably not a good idea. All things considered.'

Then he tapped her on the nose. 'It won't happen again. Good night, Lexi. Sleep well.'

She watched him stroll into the house. Sleep? After that kiss? Was he *kidding?*

CHAPTER EIGHT

'You bought me shoes?' Lexi stared at Mark open-mouthed, dangling the plain tan-leather flat sandals from one finger so that she could ogle them from every angle.

He winced, and nodded his head towards the local shop only a few feet away from the waterside restaurant where they were sitting.

'If you really hate them I won't be in the least offended. Take them back for an exchange. But the range is rather limited compared to what you're used to.'

Her eyes widened in disbelief. 'Hate them? What are you talking about?' She leaned forward over the remains of their lunch of kebab, Greek salad and hot grilled herb pitta. 'You're the first man ever to buy me shoes. This is an historic occasion. They're even the right size. I am amazingly, stunningly speechless. And I have no intention of taking them back. I may even wear them. How about that?'

He raised his water glass to her in tribute. 'The cats and I thank you for your understanding. I had a stern word with both kittens and they promise never to pee on your shoes again.' He played with a piece of bread before asking, in the most seductive voice Lexi had ever heard in her life, 'Do you really like them?'

'They are totally awesome sauce,' she murmured across the table in an equally low voice. 'Yes. I like them.'

She sat back under the sun umbrella and sipped her wine as she looked around at the harbour and the line of yachts moored in the marina in the warm bright sunshine.

'I must say, Mr Belmont, that you treat your lady guests remarkably well. A waterfront location only feet from the Mediterranean, a delicious meal, splendid local white wine–and shoes. I am impressed.'

'Thanks. I thought it was only appropriate since I have a pre-published children's author with me—that, and the small fact that we've been slaving away in that stuffy study for two days and hardly coming up for air.'

She looked at Mark over her glass.

Slaving was one way of putting it.

The constant struggle to avoid touching his body as they negotiated around each other in the small space had driven her mad with frustration.

Sometimes she could almost feel the tension between them.

But he had kept his word and not made any moves on her. And she was grateful…wasn't she? She couldn't give in to the feelings. That would mean trouble for both of them and would only end in heartbreak. She had to hold it together and fight temptation for a few more days. Just. A. Few. More. Days.

In the meantime she could enjoy his company. Memories of meals like this were going to have to sustain her on many a lonely night in a foreign hotel for a long time to come.

'It's been worth it, Mark. The book is shaping up really well, and the work we were doing this morning on your village school was lovely.' Lexi clinked her wine glass against his water beaker in a toast. 'To team work.'

'I'll drink to that. Speaking of which, I have a mission to accomplish—and you are the ideal person to advise me.'

'Ah,' Lexi replied, rubbing her hands together. 'Business or personal?'

'Personal. I have to buy a present for my nephew Freddie before I head back. Two years old and already interested in everything animal-related. I was thinking of a soft toy, but he has a room full of those already. Any ideas?'

Lexi rested her arms on the table and chuckled. 'I am no expert on toddlers. But tell me what sort of things he likes to do. What kind of games does he enjoy?'

Mark's face instantly relaxed into an expression of pure delight. 'Here. This might help. They are both total scamps, but you have to admit they're adorable.'

He dived into his trouser pocket and pulled out a state-of-the-art smartphone which made Lexi drool with envy. His fingers moved swiftly over the keyboard and a few seconds later he scooted his chair closer to hers so that she could watch the surprisingly clear images come alive on the small screen.

His body was pressed tight against hers all along one side of her capri pants and sleeveless top, and at another time and another place she would have called it a cuddle. He was so close that she could feel the golden hairs on his tanned arms against her bare skin, the heat of his breath on her neck, and the smell of his expensive designer cologne filled her head.

The overall effect was so giddying that it took her a moment to realise that he was looking at the phone rather than her, and she forced her eyes to focus on the video playing on the screen.

It was Mark. Playing with two of the cutest little boys on a sandy beach. They were making sandcastles and Mark, dressed in shorts and a T-shirt, was helping the youngest to tap the sand into his bucket with great gusto while his brother danced around with a long piece of seaweed. All three of them were laughing their heads off, and seemed to be singing silly, glorious nursery rhymes. Pure child-ish joy and delight beamed out from the brightly coloured images in front of her. They looked so happy.

Mark with his nephews. Caught in the moment. Living. Showing his love in every single laugh and smile and hug.

She glanced up at this man whose face was only inches away from hers. He was the real deal. He had taken time out from his international business to go to the beach with his nephews and simply enjoy them.

Her heart broke all over again.

Only this time it was not for Mark. It was for herself.

When had she ever done that? When had she made the effort to spend time with her mother's soon-to-be step-grandchildren or her friends' children? Or her neighbours? She hadn't. She'd chosen a job where the only children she met belonged to her clients—that way she could share their family life second-hand.

The truth of the life she had created for herself jumped out from that simple holiday video that Mark kept on his phone because he loved those boys so very much and it slapped her across the face. Hard.

She'd told herself that she wasn't ready to adopt a child as a single mum, after seeing what her mother had gone through, but the truth was simpler than that.

She was a fraud. And a liar. And a coward.

She was too scared to do it alone. Too scared to take the risk.

And here she was, trying to tell Mark Belmont how to live his life, when he was already way ahead of her in every way. He had chosen to fill his life with real children who loved him right back. Damn right.

'I think the best thing is probably to trawl the shops and throw myself on the mercy of the lovely ladies who work there.' Mark smiled, totally unaware of the turmoil roiling inside her head and her heart.

And she looked into those eyes, brimming with contentment and love for those two little boys, and thought how easy it would be just to move a couple of inches closer and kiss him the way he had kissed her under the stars. And keep kissing him to block out the hard reality of her empty life.

Bad idea. *Seriously* bad idea.

She could never give him, or any man, the children he wanted. And nothing she could do was going to change that.

Suddenly it was all too much. She needed to have some space from Mark. And fast.

'Great idea,' she gushed. 'I think I'll take a walk and meet you back here.'

Throwing her new sandals into her bag, Lexi stood up and, with one quick wave, took off down the stone wall of the harbour towards the port before Mark had a chance to reply.

White-painted wooden fishing boats with women's names lined the harbour between the marina and the commercial port, and Lexi forced herself to try and relax as she sat down on a wooden bench under the shade of a plane tree and looked out across the inlet to the open water between Paxos and Corfu.

The hydrofoil was moored at the dock and had just started loading passengers. For one split-second Lexi thought about running back to Corfu so she wouldn't have to face Mark again. All she had to do was buy a ticket and she could be on her way before he even knew she was gone.

Leaving Mark and his life and Crystal Leighton's biography and everything that came with it behind her.

Stupid, self-deluded girl. Lexi sniffed and reached for a tissue.

Other passengers had started to mill about. A taxi pulled up and a gaggle of suntanned tourists emerged, loaded down with holiday luggage, laughing and happy and enjoying their last few minutes on Paxos. Local people, children, workers, a few businessmen in suits. Just normal people going about their normal business.

And she had never felt lonelier in her life.

A stunning sailing yacht with a broad white sail drifted across the inlet on the way into the long safe harbour at Gaios, and Lexi watched as it effortlessly glided through the water.

She was simply overtired, that was all. Too many sleepless nights and tiring days. She would be fine once this assignment was finished and she was back in London with her mother.

And what then?

Tears pricked the corners of her eyes. Her mother had found a lovely man who was almost good enough for her. And even better, he had given her the grandchildren—*his* grandchildren—that she longed for, whom she already worshipped and spoilt terribly.

So where did that leave Lexi?

Alone. Directionless. Existing rather than living. Filling her life with frenetic activity and people and places and travel. On the surface it looked exciting—a perfect job for any single girl.

How had she become the very thing that she despised?

A parasite, living her life through second-hand experiences, listening to lovely people like Mark talk about their families, sharing their experiences because she was too pathetic and cowardly to have her own love affairs, her own family.

The people on that boat were free to go where they wanted. Moor up anywhere, take off when they wanted. And she felt trapped. No matter how far she travelled, or whatever she had achieved in her life, she simply could not escape the fact that she was childless and would probably be so for the rest of her life.

So why had she not done something to change that fact instead of blocking it out? When had she turned her back on her dreams and thrown them into the 'too hard to deal with' box?

She had talked to her mother about giving up full-time work and writing her own stories, but it had always seemed like a dream.

Well, the time for dreaming was over. She had her own home and could work part-time in London to pay the bills. Surely there was some publisher who'd like to work on her children's books? It would probably take years to be a financial success, but she could do it. If she was brave enough.

Couldn't she?

Lexi was so distracted by the yacht as it sailed past that when her cell phone rang she picked it up immediately, without even bothering to check the caller identity.

'Lexi? Is that you? Thank goodness. I'm so pleased to have caught up with you.'

Great. Just when she thought things couldn't get any worse. It was the talent agency. Probably checking up on her to make sure that the project was on track.

'You're not going to believe who we have lined up for your next writing assignment, Lexi. Think America's favourite grandmother and cookery writer. It's the most *amazing* opportunity, but we do need to get you out to Texas on Sunday, so you can interview all of the darling children who are staying at the ranch. Of course it'll be first class all the way and... Lexi? Are you there? Hello?'

Mark flicked down the prop stand on his scooter, whipped off his crash helmet and looked out across the road towards the hydrofoil, then breathed a huge sigh of relief

Standing on the edge of the pier, on the harbour wall, was Lexi Sloane.

And as he watched Lexi drew back her arm and threw her purple telephone with all her might over her head and into the air.

She simply stood there, panting with exertion and the heat and horror as her precious link to the outside world, her business contacts, her lifeline to business that never left her side, made a graceful arc into the sea.

It hit the waves with a slight splosh and was gone.

Well, that was interesting.

Lexi hardly noticed that someone had come to sit next to her on the bench until he stretched out his legs and she saw the sharp crease on his smart navy trousers, and the black crash helmet cradled on his knee.

'Hi,' she said.

'Hello,' Mark replied. 'I didn't have much luck in the shops so I thought I'd join you, instead. Much more entertaining.'

They sat in silence, watching the hydrofoil crew help passengers onto the deck.

Lexi lifted her head and frowned, as though she had just woken up from a deep sleep.

'Did I just throw my phone into the sea?'

'Yes. I watched you do it from the car park. For a casual overarm technique it made a very nice curve for the few seconds it was airborne. Have you ever thought of playing cricket? Not much of a splash, though.'

'Oh. I was hoping I had imagined that bit. No chance I could get it back, I suppose?'

'Sorry. Your phone is probably covered by about thirty feet of salt water by now.'

'Right. Thirty feet.'

Mark sidled up to her on the bench. 'When I take an awkward call I often find it better to wait a few moments before replying. How about you?'

She shook her head. 'You see what people do to me? They make my head spin so fast that I throw my phone, that I need for my job and has all my numbers, into the sea.' She gesticulated towards the open water. 'There's probably a law against polluting the Mediterranean with small electrical items. Perhaps you could direct me to the local police station? Because I have to tell you, handing myself in and spending some time in solitary confinement sounds pretty good to me right now.'

She swallowed hard but no more words would form through the pain in her throat.

'Attractive though that option might sound, I have an alternative suggestion. I have a spare phone and a number of spare bedrooms which you are welcome to use any time you like. And I still owe you dessert. If you are available?'

'Available? Oh, yes, I am available. I'm always ready to step in at a moment's notice when they can't find anyone else. Why not? After all, I don't have a life.'

'Don't say that. You know it isn't true.'

'Do I? Then why is it that I choose to live through other people's experiences of a happy family life, and other women's children? No, Mark, I do it because I want to for-get for just those few days that I am never going to have children of my own. But it's crushing me. It is totally crushing me.'

And then lovely Lexi, totally in control as ever, burst into hysterical tears.

CHAPTER NINE ·

Lexi sat back on the sofa with her eyes closed. The patio doors were wide open and a gentle breeze cooled the hot air. It was evening now, and the only sounds were the soft hum of the air-conditioning unit on the wall, the cicadas in the olive grove and somewhere in the village some chickens being put away for the night.

The gentle glug of wine being poured into a crystal goblet filtered through Lexi's hazed senses, and she opened her eyes just in time to see Mark smiling at her.

'Feeling better now?'

She nodded. 'Almost human.'

And she meant it. She'd enjoyed a luxurious bath, with some amazingly expensive products Mark's sister had left behind from her last visit, and was now being cosseted and pampered by a handsome man.

The day was turning out a lot better than she had expected.

'I'm sorry about what happened at the harbour earlier, Mark. I don't usually burst into tears. But do you remember we'd been talking about how your mum had given up her career for a few years when you were small? So that she could take you to school in the morning and take you to see your friends and make cakes for your birthday parties?'

'Yes, of course. We loved it.'

'Well, sitting on that harbour this afternoon it hit me out of the blue that somewhere deep inside my head I know I'm never going to have that life—and like a fool I've been living through other people's stories.'

'What do you mean other people? You have a perfectly good life of your own.'

'Do I? All those celebrities I work with? I've been making a life for myself through their love affairs, their pregnancies, their children, their families—the good and bad and all the joy that comes with being a parent. That's what hurts. I've been using their lives as some sort of replacement for the family I'll never have—for the children I'll never meet. And that's not just sad, it's pathetic. Wake-up call. *Huge.* Cue tears.'

Her voice faded away and she tried to give Mark a smile as he kissed her on the forehead and pressed his chin into her hair.

'I think you would make a wonderful mother.'

Lexi squeezed her lips together and shrugged her shoulder. 'That's not going to happen Mark. That illness I was telling you about? I was diagnosed with leukaemia two months after my tenth birthday.'

Mark inhaled sharply, and his body seemed to freeze into position next to her on the sofa but he said nothing.

'I know. Not good. But I was lucky. I lived in central London and had a very quick diagnosis and treatment at one of the best children's hospitals in the world. I was in hospital for what seemed like forever. It was…painful and difficult to endure. My mum was there every day, and my dad phoned me now and then, but I knew he would never come.'

Her head dropped onto her chest and she twiddled the ring on her right hand. She paused and took a moment to compose herself before going on, and to his credit, Mark didn't interrupt her but gently stroked the back of her hand, as if reassuring her that he was there and ready to listen to anything she had to tell him.

'The day I was due to be discharged from hospital I remember being so excited. I can't tell you how wonderful it was to see my own home again, and my own room with all my things in it. Best of all, my dad was there. Waiting at the front door. With his suitcases. For a few precious moments I thought we were going on holiday somewhere warm, so I could get better. And then he closed the door, and he wouldn't let me hug him or kiss him because he said I was still getting better and he had a cold. Then he turned to my mother and told her that he had met someone on location in Mexico and had decided to make a fresh start with this girl and her daughter. He picked up his suitcases, opened the door, walked down the path to a huge black limousine and jumped inside.'

Her brows twisted and she had difficulty continuing. 'I couldn't walk very fast, and my mother... She was running after the limo, screaming his name over and over. Telling him to stop, begging him to come back. But the car didn't stop. It went faster and faster. When I caught up with her she was kneeling in the road, watching the car speed round the corner, taking my dad away from us.'

Bitter hot tears pricked the corners of her eyes and Lexi blinked them away.

Mark sat next to her on the sofa and wrapped his arm around her shoulders. 'You don't have to talk about it.'

'Yes, I do,' she answered. 'Because the past never goes away. There's always something there to remind you, and just when you think you're on a happy track and can forget about it and move on—*smack!* There it is again. Staring you in the face.'

'How did you ever get over that betrayal?'

'Oh, Mark. You never get over it. My mother taught me to focus on the best memories we had as a family. But she never really understood why I felt so guilty, and that guilt consumed me for years. Until I saw what he was really like.'

'You felt *guilty*? I don't understand why the ten-year-old Lexi would feel guilty about her father leaving.'

'Can't you see? I was the one who got the cancer. I was the one who forced my dad to have an affair with a beautiful actress on a movie set because it was too upsetting and painful for him to come back and deal with my illness and pain. I was the one who drove him to find another daughter who was prettier than me and healthier and cleverer and more talented and...'

Her voice gave way, unable to sustain the emotion any more.

'Parents aren't supposed to abandon their children,' Mark whispered. 'Sometimes I regret going to university in America. I loved being with my friends in a wonderful country where the world seemed open and full of opportunities to explore and to do business. I just forgot that my family needed me back in England. I could never have imagined that one day my mother wouldn't be there at the airport to take me home. We missed so many weekends and holidays together.'

'Young people leave home and follow their hearts and careers. Your mother knew that. Her little boy had grown up, with his own life to lead. She must have been so proud of you and what you've achieved.' Her voice faltered and she stroked his face with her fingertip as she went on. 'We're so very similar in many ways. We're both survivors. I came through cancer. I watched my mother going through torment as my father cheated on us both, then struggle to balance life as a single working mother with a sickly child.'

'Is she happy now?'

Lexi nodded. 'Very. She's taking a chance and getting married again. Brave woman!' She grinned at Mark. 'I think that's why finding out Adam cheated on me was so hard. In the past I could have laughed it off. Joked that it was his loss. But somehow this time it really did feel as though I was the one who'd lost out. He didn't have the courage to tell me what the real problem was. Apparently he wanted children after all.'

'Had you spoken to him about children?'

'Of course. That was why I was in the hospital. Having tests to find out if there was anything I could do to improve my chances. I do have more options than I ever thought possible, but they made it clear that the treatments are very gruelling and there's no guarantee of success.'

'So it didn't bother him that you couldn't have his children?'

Lexi turned and looked at Mark. There had been a touch of coldness in his voice.

'He said he would be happy to adopt at some point, but it was never going to happen. Adam was doing loads of location work, and I was travelling more and more. These past few months we hardly saw each other.'

'I'm sorry that it didn't work out. It's hard on you. So very hard.'

'Perhaps that's why I want to write children's stories— I can make up a happy ending and send a child to sleep knowing that all is well with the world and they are safe and happy, with loving parents who care for them. Maybe all of the love I have will filter through to those children

I'll never get to meet or hug through my words on the page.'

Lexi swallowed down her anguish and looked into his eyes.

Fatal mistake.

It meant she was powerless to resist when Mark shifted closer to her and reached up to hold her face in his hands, gently caressing her skin, his eyes locked on to hers.

And then he tilted his head to kiss her.

His full mouth moved in delicious slow curves against hers, and she closed her eyes to luxuriate in the tender kiss of this warm, gentle man she'd soon have to say goodbye to.

She put her arms around his neck and kissed him back, pressing hotter and deeper against his mouth, the pace of her breathing almost matching his. It was a physical wrench when his lips left hers and she gasped a breath of air to cool the heat that threatened to overwhelm her.

'I was hoping there was another very good reason why you might want to stay on Paxos instead of heading back to London so soon,' he whispered in her ear, before his lips started moving down towards her throat, nuzzling the little space under her ear.

At which point the sensible part of her brain admitted defeat and decided to have some fun, instead.

'You mean apart from the excellent accommodation and room service?' She batted her eyelashes.

'Absolutely,' he replied with a grin. 'I'm talking about the full package of optional extras here.' He tapped her twice on the end of her nose and lowered his voice. 'I don't have to go back for a few days. And there's nowhere else I would rather be than right here with you. Take a chance, Lexi. Stay. Let me get to know you better. Who knows? You might like me back.'

He shifted slightly and looked away. 'Besides, the cats would miss you terribly if you left now. They're waiting to—'

Lexi silenced him with one fingertip pressed against his lips.

'It's okay. You had me at the word *cats*.'

Lexi turned over and tried to find a comfy position. Only something solid and man-shaped was in the way. She cracked one eye open, then smiled with deep satisfaction.

Warm morning sunlight was flooding into the living room and reflecting back from the cream-coloured walls in a golden glow that made everything seem light and fresh.

It had not been a dream.

She really had just spent the night on the sofa with Mark Belmont.

At some point Mark had suggested going into the bedroom, but that would have destroyed this precious connection, which was so special and unique. She didn't need to take her clothes off and jump on him to show how much she cared.

Lexi snuggled into the warmth of his chest, and Mark's arm wrapped around her shoulders and drew her closer into his body.

Lexi's hand pressed against the long tantalising strip of bare chest she'd created by unbuttoning his shirt in the night. She closed her eyes and moved her forehead against the soft fabric of the shirt, inhaling its fragrance. It was musky, deep and sensuous, and totally, totally unique to this remarkable man.

'I have a question,' she murmured, her eyes closed.

A deep chuckle came from inside Mark's chest, and Lexi could feel the vibrations of his voice under her fingertips. It was weird that such a simple sensation made her heart sing with delight at the fact that she could be here, in this moment, enjoying this connection. No matter how fleeting or temporary it might be this was very special, and she knew that Mark felt the same.

'Out with it,' he growled, 'but it had better be important to disturb my beauty sleep at this hour of the morning.'

'Indeed,' she replied, trying not to give him the satisfaction of a grin. But it was too hard to resist, and she slid out of his arms and propped herself up on her elbow to look at Mark's face.

'Do you know that you have two grey hairs on your chest?' she asked in a semi-serious voice. 'And one just here.' Her forefinger stroked down the side of Mark's chin against the soft stubble, then tapped very gently at the offending hair.

'Are you offering a personal grooming service?' He smiled.

'Oh, if required a freelance writer should be ready to carry out any duties necessary to complete a task. No matter how odd or dangerous or *icky* the task.'

'I had no idea,' he said gravely, 'of the horror you must face on a daily basis.'

'Explorers going out into the unknown,' Lexi replied, her left hand making a sweep of the room. 'Armed only with a designer wardrobe and a make-up bag. Not for the faint-hearted. And that's just the boys.'

She lowered her head and rubbed her nose against his. 'It is, of course, essential that a writer should investigate local customs, which must be observed wherever possible,' she whispered in a low, sensual voice as her lips made circles around his mouth. 'So important. Don't you think?'

'Absolutely,' he replied, his mouth moving down the side of her neck.

Lexi closed her eyes and lifted her chin so that he could fit more closely into her throat.

'Were you thinking of any in particular?'

'Actually, I was… Oh, that's good.' Lexi sucked in a breath as Mark nuzzled aside the neck of her stretchy T-shirt and started kissing along the length of her collar-bone. 'I was thinking about how people celebrate important dates in the year.' Her words came out in a rush as her breath suddenly seemed to be much in demand. 'Wedding anniversaries, Christmas, Easter and…' She slid down a gulp of anxiety and uncertainty before she said the word which would either be a horrible mistake or a wonderful way to connect them even more.

'And…?' a low husky voice breathed into her ear.

Lexi opened her eyes. She wanted to see how Mark responded to what she was about to say.

'Family birthdays,' she replied gently, hardly daring to say the words in case they brought back bad as well as wonderful memories. 'Like today, for example. Your mum's birthday.'

Mark was silent for a moment, and then he smiled and lay back on the sofa cushions. He looked at her—really looked at her—his eyes scanning her face, looking for something. For a few terrible moments Lexi felt that she had made a terrible mistake. But the words were out and couldn't be taken back.

'Clever girl. Mum would have been sixty today.'

He stretched out the full length of the sofa with a sigh, his head on her lap and one of his arms flailing onto the floor, his eyes staring at the ceiling. Mark seemed so totally natural and relaxed in her presence that it made her heart sing.

'Would she have hated turning sixty?' she asked quietly. 'Or would she have taken it in stride? Just another day?'

Mark was silent for a moment, before he looked up at her and gave a small shrug.

'Hated it. With a passion. I remember her fiftieth birth-day party in London. She went to the gym every day for six months. Facials, Botox, hairdressers galore. Trips to Paris for flattering outfits. The works. Just so she'd look amazing in the photographs on that one night. And it worked. I remember those photos appearing across the world in every newspaper and gossip magazine. Crystal Leighton looking ten years younger. Or was it twenty? She made headlines at that party. She even announced a new contract with a make-up company at the same time. All part of the plan to revitalise her career and keep her name on the front page.'

He broke into a lopsided loving grin. 'She loved being the centre of attention at big events. The adulation, the crowds, flashguns, photographers. Mum could sign autographs for an hour and not get bored with it. There was no way she'd ever allow herself to be anything less than spectacular.' His grin faded. 'But that was in public.'

He reached up and pushed a lock of her hair back behind the ear with two fingertips, as though he'd been doing it all his life, and she revelled in the simple touch of his skin against hers.

'Crystal Leighton was totally professional in every way when she was at work. But her fans forgot that when she got home at night she took off her war paint and designer clothing and Crystal Leighton became Baroness Belmont. Wife and mother. And I don't think anyone truly saw her for the remarkable woman that she was.'

'Then tell them. Help them to understand.'

Mark started to sigh with exasperation, but Lexi pressed her hand hard against his chest and he stilled under her touch.

'You and your family are the only people who knew who she truly was. And now you have the power to celebrate that wonderful woman who was your mother.'

'I don't—'

'I know.' Lexi smiled. 'You don't want to hurt your family by revealing how very unhappy she was at the end. That's why I'm here. I'm helping you write a memoir. Not a dry list of dates and all the films she was in—anyone can get that from the internet. No. This is going to be a personal memoir.'

Lexi tapped a finger against his forehead. 'I want to release all those wonderful stories and precious memories you have inside your head and make this a *real* memoir which only you and your family could write. That's what is going to make this book so remarkable and real. And that's how you're going to give your mother the best birthday present she could ever have had. Because you know homemade presents are always the best.'

'A birthday present? I like that idea. Can we have birthday cake and bubbly?'

'I'm astonished that you have to ask. And a monster-sized birthday card. Just tell me what kind of cake takes your fancy and I'm your girl.'

'My girl? Is that right? Well, how could I possibly resist an offer like that?' His face relaxed and he blinked several times. 'Lemon drizzle. She liked lemon-drizzle sponge. With a dusting of icing sugar. No fancy cakestands or anything. Just an ordinary lemon-drizzle sponge. And a gallon of boiling hot tea to wash it down with. I'd completely forgotten about that until this minute.'

'Crystal Belmont's lemon cake,' Lexi replied in a far-away voice. 'Oh, my. That's lovely.'

Lexi sat up so quickly that she felt dizzy, and Mark's

head dropped onto the cushion. 'That's it! You are *so* clever.' She bent forward and touched her lips against his.

'It's been said before, but not frequently in this particular situation. Please explain before my head explodes.'

'The title for the memoir! I've been racking my brain all week to come up with an interesting title which will make your book stand out on the shelves.' She beamed down at Mark and shook her head slowly from side to side. 'I hate to say I was right, but sometimes I amaze myself. You have everything you need to write this story inside your head. My job is to make it into a book. And I can't wait to get started.'

Lexi flung back the light cover from her legs, swung her body off the sofa, and was on her feet and reaching for her sandals in an instant.

'Right. Time to make a list. So much to do and so little time.'

'Lexi?'

She looked back at Mark, still lying flat on the sofa with a certain smile on his face.

'Can't we do that later?' he implored. 'Much later?' And he waggled his eyebrows at her.

She sniffed at his cheeky grin. 'Work now, cuddle later, you scamp. You have a lot to do today. I'll get the coffee started while you're in the shower—then straight to the computer so we can start dictation. This is going to be *so* much fun!'

Lexi skipped out of the door before Mark could grab her and employ his best powers of persuasion to make her stay.

He could hear her humming happily as the plain leather sandals he'd bought her clapped along the tiled floor towards the ground-floor bathroom.

Telling Lexi about his mum's birthday parties? That

was new. But maybe she was right? Maybe there was a chance he *could* write this biography as a celebration of her life and make it a positive, happy thing, with only a tinge of sadness.

Mark linked his hands under his head and lay back as the sun filled the room with bright morning light. It was going to be another hot sunny day on Paxos, and from deep inside his body came a warm feeling of contentment that bubbled up and emerged as a smile that surprised his face.

He had slept for eight hours straight on a very uncomfortable sofa with a woman in his arms. For the first time in many years he hadn't snapped awake to reach for some electronic gadget and check his email, compulsively making sure he hadn't missed an important message about the business while he wasted time sleeping.

He could hear Lexi moving around in the kitchen. The hiss of water into a kettle. Cups rattling on the worktop and metal spoons hitting the olive wood tray. Was this the soundtrack to happiness he'd been looking for all his life? Or simply the joyful noise that came with sharing your home with this whirlwind of a girl?

He had found someone he wanted to be with in the last place on the planet he'd ever expected to. In this wonderful house that held so many memories of his mother and happy childhood holidays.

How could he have known that the path to happiness would lead right back to where he'd once been so happy? How ironic was that?

Belmont Investments and the manor were not important any longer.

This was where he wanted to be. *Needed* to be. With Lexi.

And now she was here. And he felt an overwhelming, all-powerful connection.

Finally. It had happened. He'd known lust and attraction. But this sensation was so new, so startling, that the great Mark Belmont floundered.

He was falling for Lexi Sloane.

'Mark?' Lexi popped her head around the door. 'Perhaps you should telephone your dad. He might need to hear your voice today of all days.'

And then she was gone, back to the kitchen before he had a chance to answer, singing along to a pop song, oblivious of the fact that she had thrown him a bomb and he'd caught it single-handed.

Telephone his dad? On his mother's birthday?

Oh, Lexi.

This lovely girl really had no idea whatsoever just how much it would take for him to lift the telephone and make that call. What would he say to his father? What *could* he say?

All his father cared about was the heritage of the estate and how his only remaining son was going to ensure their lineage was carried on. And Mark's failure to get married and produce an heir was starting to become a problem.

Mark swung his legs over the sofa and ran his hands down over the creases in his trousers.

His engagement had been a catastrophe—a disaster meant to placate his parents. He knew that his father blamed him for letting his fiancée go.

Failure. Yet again.

And here he was, falling for a girl who couldn't give him children. Couldn't give him the heir that he was supposed to provide.

More failure.

What was he doing with Lexi? What was he *thinking?*

The answer was only too clear. He wasn't thinking at

all. He was living and reacting and loving life, and he had Lexi to thank for that.

It didn't matter what happened in the future. It didn't matter one jot. He'd have to deal with the consequences when they happened. They both lived in London. They were both single. And, unless he had completely misread the signals, she felt the same way about him. And that was too special to give up.

Since Edmund had died Mark's life had been filled with obligation and duty. He loved his family too much to let them down. But Lexi was right. They were both living second-hand lives.

All that mattered was right here and right now.

Living in the moment. He quite liked the sound of that.

Without a second's further delay, Mark stretched up to his full height and headed off to the kitchen. Time to entertain the cats and drink coffee on the terrace with the woman he simply couldn't bear to be apart from.

CHAPTER TEN

'You have a whole hour to titivate yourself,' Mark joked, jumping into Lexi's hire car and cranking down the anti-cat-invasion window, 'while I'm on my perilous, swash-buckling mission to track down two bottles of champagne and the local version of lemon-drizzle cake. I'll be back with the swag before you know it.'

Lexi stuck her head through the window and kissed him swiftly but firmly on the lips. 'You'd better be.' She grinned. 'I have my favourite dress ready and waiting, and matching shoes that the cats haven't peed on yet.' She winked at him. 'It's going to be a lovely birthday party. And please bring back more doughnuts for breakfast.'

She kissed him again, and again and one more time for luck, before waggling her nose against his with a giggle, then standing back and waving as he sped off down the road towards the biggest town on the island.

Lexi stood and watched the car until it turned the cor-ner onto the main road, carrying inside it the man she was already longing to see again. She felt as though part of her was somehow missing without Mark by her side.

The cool and unhappy man she had met only a few days earlier was gone, replaced by a remarkable, talented, gentle-hearted man who loved to laugh and enjoy himself.

He knew her faults, her history and he certainly knew

about her dad. And yet he still wanted to be with her. Which was so very amazing that it made her head spin.

And now she had a lovely birthday-party dinner to look forward to, followed by drinks on the terrace watching the sun go down, and then maybe a little stargazing. If they weren't otherwise occupied.

Delicious!

Was it any wonder that she adored him? Perhaps a little too much, and way too fast... But she adored him all the same.

Well... Now it was her turn to dazzle and give him a treat in return.

Lexi skipped up the steps to the house, waving at the sun-kissed cats on the way, and took the stairs to the first floor two at a time.

Clothes first. Then hair and miracle make-up. Mark Belmont would not know what had hit him—because tonight he was going to get the full works.

Let the titivation ensue.

Twenty minutes later Lexi was still humming a pop song under her breath as she jogged from the shower to her bedroom and flung open the wardrobe door.

Her designer cream-lace lingerie would have to do. But she hadn't been kidding about her favourite dress.

No wild patterns, flowers or multi-coloured designs this time. Just a completely sweet confection of flowing gold lace over a plain cream-silk shift dress picked out by her mother with her expert eye.

Elegant. Understated. Knockout.

She had only worn the dress once before, at the Valentine's Day party when her mother had announced her engagement. Somehow it had never seemed lively or colourful enough for any of the movie functions in Hong Kong, but now—in this villa, on this tiny island, with only Mark and the cats to see it—yes. She was glad she had hauled it through so many airport departure lounges.

The cream silk felt cool and luxurious against her moisturised skin. Sensuous and smooth and just what she needed. She smoothed down the lace overskirt and admired herself in the full-length mirror, turning from side to side for a few seconds before smiling and giving herself a quick nod in admiration.

'Not too bad, girl,' she whispered to herself with a wink. 'You'll do nicely.'

But now for the killer touch. Lexi reached into a shoe bag with the name of a famous Asian shoe designer on the front and pulled out a pair of pale gold kitten-heeled satin mules.

They were limo shoes and always would be. No excuses. These shoes were designed for fine wool and silk carpets, not country stone patios, and had cost more than she'd ever paid for shoes in her life even if they had been on sale. But she didn't care.

So what if they'd only ever seen red carpets before now? She was wearing them for Mark, who was all that mattered.

A little giggle of happiness bubbled up from deep inside her chest and Lexi bit her lower lip in pleasure as she slipped on the mules and posed in front of the mirror.

It had been such a long time since she had felt so light. So joyous. So very happy.

Yes. That was it. *Happy.*

This was so strange. Before this week, if anyone had asked if she was happy she would have answered with some glib statement about her magical, awesome life.

Not now. Not any longer. In a few short days Mark had shown her what real happiness could be like.

Until now she'd been living her life through other people's experiences, and now it was her turn to love. Not simple contentment, not settling for the best she could but true happiness with someone she loved.

Lexi inhaled sharply and pressed her fingertips to her throat.

Loved?

Was that it? Was that why she felt that she had been waiting for Mark all her life?

Breathing out slowly, Lexi tottered the few steps across to Crystal's library and ran her fingers down the rows of photographs Mark had chosen to feature in the opening chapters of the book.

They'd spent three glorious days together, laughing and chatting, and all the while Mark had dictated wonderful anecdotes, happy memories of his mother's life and the people she'd met, the things she'd done.

If only he could come to terms with the sad moments. Then it would be a remarkable biography. And she was happy to help.

Happy to do anything that meant she spent as much time with him as she could.

Looking at the photographs now, she could see that each image captured a moment in time when the young Belmont family had been happy together. Before things had changed and they'd lost that easy familiarity.

Her fingers rested on the photo she'd picked up on her first morning at the villa. The schoolboy Mark and his brother Edmund, arms around each other, muddy, happy and proud on the football pitch.

There was so much love shining out from the flat matte surface.

Edmund the older brother. Heir to the estate. The next Baron Belmont.

A shiver of unease ran across Lexi's shoulders and she

scanned the photographs, looking for some sign of where things had changed.

And there it was. Mark must have been in his early twenties when this photograph had been taken at some movie award ceremony. He was standing next to Crystal, who looked stunning, but that spark, that easy, relaxed expression that Lexi had come to know on Mark, was missing. Snuffed out.

It was more than grief at losing his brother. It was as though the heavy weight of being the only son and heir to the Belmont estate was sitting on his shoulders, pressing him down.

It truly was a shame that Cassie's boys would never inherit the title.

An icy feeling quivered and roiled inside Lexi's stomach and she slumped down onto the nearest hard chair.

Bad choice. Because the chair faced a small round mirror on the wall opposite. And as she glanced at her reflection all the energy and fun and joy of the day drifted away, leaving behind the cold, hard reality she'd managed to stuff deep into the 'too difficult to handle today' box.

Shame that she'd chosen this minute to let it out.

Because suddenly her lovely dress and shoes felt like a sad joke.

She did not have any future with Mark. How could she when she was unable to give him the son he needed to carry on his family name and title?

Sniffing away the tears, she stared at photo after photo through blurred vision.

His family meant everything to him.

It was so unfair. So totally unfair. Just when she thought she'd found the love of her life. Staying with Mark, loving Mark, sharing her life with Mark would force him to decide between his family and her.

And she couldn't do that to him. She loved him too much to put him in that position.

What was she going to do?

The sun was already low in the apricot-tinged sky when Mark pushed through the cypress and olive trees onto the secluded circle of stones facing the cliffs and the open sea.

But at that moment not even the view from this special place his mother had used as her escape could compare with the lovely woman sitting so quietly with her eyes closed and her head leaning back on the sun-warmed bench.

It staggered him that one look at her beautiful face could send his senses into a stomach-clenching, mind-reeling, heart-thumping overdrive.

What was it about her that made him feel like a schoolboy on a first date?

His heart raced just at the sight of her, and it was as if he'd dreamt this marvellous creature up out of his imagination—because she was too special to be real.

Lexi's skin and dress were lit by golden and pink sunlight, creating the illusion that she was lit from within, that she was the source of the light. Shades of gold. Apricot and pink.

She looked stunning.

No amount of clever studio lighting would be able to recreate this unique combination of place and time, and Mark instinctively knew that this image would stay locked in the safe and secure place where he kept his most treasured possessions: wonderful memories of love and happiness forever.

Not in printed photographs which could be recreated inside the pages of a biography for others to read. But inside his head and heart, where the real Mark Belmont had been kept safe until now.

Waiting for someone to release him from the constraints he'd made for himself to get him through the obligations he'd accepted for his family.

That someone was Lexi Sloane.

And he loved her for it.

Time to step up and prove that he was good enough for her.

But as he moved the dry pine needles covering the stones on the gravel path crunched beneath his smart shoes, and her eyes flicked open and she looked at him.

And in that one single glance any doubt he might have had was wiped away.

He was in love. Not for the first time—but for the last.

She was the one he wanted. For good.

Lexi stretched her arms out so that they rested on the back of the bench and smiled. Waiting for him to speak. As he came closer he saw something more than relaxed confidence in that smile. Confusion, regret. And apprehension. She was nervous.

Oh, yes. He recognised *that* look only too well. His stomach was suddenly ice.

She was leaving him and she didn't know how to do it without hurting his feelings. He was grateful for that sensitivity, but it wouldn't make the next few minutes any easier.

Her fingers started to curl into tight knots of tension, but she instantly blocked the move, stretched out her fingers and turned it into the casual brush of a stray dry leaf from the stonework as he strolled closer.

'Hello,' she said with a small smile. 'I hope you don't mind, but I couldn't bear to miss my last sunset. Looking for me?'

Here it comes, he thought, *and she doesn't know how to handle it.*

'I'm not used to being stood up,' Mark replied. 'Came as quite a shock. Especially since my mission was completely successful, and our party food is ready and waiting back at the villa.'

She raised her eyebrows. 'Congratulations. I…er… waited for you.' Her fingers waved in the direction of the main road. 'But I got lonely.'

He winced. 'Ah. Thanks for the note. It was good to know that you hadn't been kidnapped by pirates or called back to write some other biography at the last minute. Sorry I was late. I was tied up on the phone to Cassie, trying to organise a surprise thank-you present for you.'

Her mind reeled with the impact of what he'd said, and she slid back down onto the hard stone bench and looked up at him in astonishment.

'A thank-you present? I don't expect a present, Mark. I'm just doing my job—your publisher is already paying me a great deal of money to be here.'

'Then think of it as a bonus. From the family.'

'The family? You mean the family who doesn't know who my father is? *That* family?'

Mark tapped his forefinger against his lower lip as he nodded, and then broke into a smile at her stunned face. 'Yup. I loved what you said about having your own writer's cottage, hidden away in the woodland. Well, I have woodland on the Belmont estate. Beech woods, oak, maple and hornbeam. And they are beautiful. Stunningly beautiful, in fact. Which got me thinking that clever people who write children's stories—' he tapped her on the end of the nose '—might care to test out one of the cottages to see if they work as country retreats for artists and writers. What do you say, Lexi? Are you willing to take the risk and give it a go?'

In the absolute stillness of the secret place the air was filled with the sound of nature: flying insects in the olive groves on the other side of the footpath, and birds calling on the clifftops where they nested. But Lexi did not hear the sea-birds. She was way too busy fighting to keep breathing in a controlled manner.

Because they both knew that he wasn't just talking about renting a cottage. Oh, no.

Mark lowered his body onto the bench next to her and stretched out his long legs towards the sea wall, his splayed fingers only inches from hers.

One side of his throat was lit rosy pink by the fading sun as he twisted his body to face her, apparently oblivious to the damage he was causing to the fine fabric of his trousers, which stretched to accommodate the muscled thighs below.

'What do you say?' he repeated, his blue eyes locked on her face, his voice low and intense, anxious. 'Would you be interested in moving into my world? Say yes. Say you'll run away from the city and come and write your children's stories in one of my cottages. Trust me, I will make sure that your new home has everything you could possibly want. It'll be so perfect that you'll never want to leave.'

Trust him? Trust him with her life? Her future? Her love?

'Why me?' she asked, her voice almost a whisper.

His response was to slide his long, strong fingers between hers and lock them there. Tight. A wide grin of delight and happiness cracked his face.

'For the last five months I've done everything I can to avoid going back to my home. You've helped me see that

Belmont Manor is where I belong. I can't run away from home forever. But it's missing one thing which would make it truly special.' He flashed a cheeky smile. 'The woman I'm looking at right now.'

Her dream of finishing her stories.

Her own home with someone who loved her.

This amazing man was offering her the chance she had been waiting for, working towards every second since she'd started writing down her grandmother's children stories all those years ago. This man she'd met only a few days ago, yet she felt she'd known him all her life.

He was holding her dream out to her, confident that she could do it. All she had to do was say yes and it would be hers.

Lexi leaned back and her sides pressed against the stone.

She inhaled a deep breath, trying to process words when his body was only inches away from her own, leaning towards her, begging her to hold him, kiss him, caress him.

She swallowed hard down a burning throat and tried to form a sensible answer.

'Belmont Manor? I don't understand. I thought you couldn't wait to leave your father and run your own life in the city?'

'It dawned on me that I have to *talk* to my family about the important things in my life now and then. Strange concept. But I'm getting used to the idea and it might just work. And of course there is one final reason why you are the only writer I would ask to test out my writers' retreat.'

Lexi let out a long slow breath as his fingertips moved over her forehead and curled around the layers of her hair before caressing her neck in slow, languorous circles.

'Why is that?' she whispered, almost frightened at what he might say next.

'It's not every day that I get the chance to make a girl's

dream come true. I want to read your stories to my nephews one day. Will you let me into your life to help you do that?'

Suddenly it was all too much for her to take in.

Let her into his life? Make her dream a reality because her cared for her?

She looked out towards the distant horizon, where the calm ocean formed a line with the apricot sky, and was instantly transported into her happy dream of what life could be like. Writing in her little wooden retreat in the forest all day. And then maybe the tantalising prospect of being with Mark every evening, sharing their lives, their dreams and their hopes for the future.

Future. The reality of what he was proposing hit her hard.

Idiot girl! Who was she kidding? They *had* no future.

By looking down and taking both of Mark's hands in hers she managed to regain some composure so words became possible.

'This is a wonderful offer, and I'm sure that I would love it there, but you know I have to work as a contract writer to pay the bills, and I can't accept your charity. Or your pity.'

His fingers meshed into hers and he raised one hand to his lips, gently kissed her knuckles before replying.

'Last I heard writers can work from home and be quite successful. You're so talented, Lexi—you can do this. I know you can.'

The pressure in her chest was almost too much to bear as she looked into his face and saw that he meant it. He believed in her!

'You'd do that? You'd put up with having me hanging around the place? Even with my horrible taste in music and annoying habits?'

'If it meant I could be with you? In a heartbeat.'

Mark's words seem to echo inside her head. Her chest and her whole body were filled with their overwhelming joy and deep love.

She forced herself to look up into his face, and what she saw there took her breath away. Any doubt that this man cared about her was wiped away in an instant.

No pity, no excuses, no apologies. Just a smouldering inner fire. Focused totally on her.

'And now you've gone quiet. I find this worrying,' he joked.

'I can't think, Mark. This is all too new and terrifying. I need to try and get my head around what's going on, make sense of it all. Can you understand that?'

'What's going on is that you have come to mean a great deal to me—more than I could ever have expected. Not for one minute did I believe that anyone could reach inside me and open up my heart, make me vulnerable again.' He grabbed hold of both her hands and held them tight against his chest. 'It's taken me years to build up so many layers of defences. This suit of armour I've created is even more impressive than the one standing in the hall at Belmont Manor. But I needed it so no one could hurt me and break my heart again. And then you walked into my life—my empty, busy and on-the-surface so-successful life—and you smiled at me. And ever since that moment my life hasn't been my own any more. It just took a while for the message to get through.'

He must have seen the terror in her eyes and felt her fast breath on his neck, because Mark took a second before smiling and lowering his voice.

'And now I'm doing it again. Rushing ahead of myself just to keep pace with you.'

He kissed her fingertips one by one.

'Don't you understand, Lexi? You've taken me hostage.

Heart and soul and mind. You've become part of me. And you feel the same. I hope—no, I *know* that I am part of you, so please don't try and deny it. Because I can see it in your eyes and feel it in your touch.'

And suddenly she couldn't stand to look into his eyes and say what she had to. It was just too painful.

His presence was so powerful, so dominating, that she slid her fingers away from his and pushed herself off the stone bench and across a few steps to the cliff wall.

Sucking in cool air, she looked down the steep bank towards the sea below, to the crashing waves on the boulders at the foot of the tall white cliff to her right.

She could jump into Mark's arms and leap into the deep, warm ocean of life with him, knowing that he would hold her up and not let her drown. But one day the waves of his obligations would crash over their heads and they would both drown in a sea of bitterness and despair from which there was no going back.

She couldn't bear it. Not when Mark had a chance to find someone else and have a happy married life with children to carry his name and his heritage to more generations.

She loved this man too much to allow him to sacrifice everything he held sacred. Just to be with her.

The very thought that he'd offered her that amazing gift filled her heart and soul with happiness and a sweet contentment that they'd at least shared these few precious days together. That was going to have to be enough.

Mark was standing behind her now, and she felt the light touch of his hands on each side of her waist.

Lexi immediately pulled his hands closer to her body, so that she could grasp them to her chest as it rose and fell. His knuckles rested on the exposed skin of her throat and neck, and the heat of the delicate touch and the gentle pressure of his chest against the back of her dress warmed her body as nothing ever had before.

He was the flame that had set her world on fire, and she knew beyond any measure of doubt that no man could ever touch her heart the way Mark had.

He was the love of her life.

Which was precisely why she was going to have to walk away from him.

All she had to do now was turn around and tell him to his face.

Slowly, inch by inch, she lowered his hands and slid her fingers out, one by one, until they were only in contact at the fingertips, before turning around within the circle of his arms.

But she couldn't do it. She surrendered to her desire for one last time and pressed her head onto his chest, her arms around his neck, hanging on for dear life, pulling his head lower.

His eyes flickered at her touch, and she had to blink away tears as his nose pressed against her cheek, his mouth nuzzling her upper lip as his fingers moved back to clasp the back of her head, drawing her closer to him.

His hard body was against her, rock-solid, safe and secure, and so loving that the overall effect was more than intoxicating.

And then his mouth was pressing hotter and hotter onto hers, his pulse racing below the fine cloth as he pushed her lips apart and explored her mouth. One of his hands made slow circles on the small of her back, then higher, while the other caressed the skin at the base of her skull so gently that she thought she would go mad with wanting Mark so much, needing him to know how much she cared.

She felt carried away on a sea of love and deep connection that she could happily drown in and not regret for a moment.

Maybe that was why she broke away first, leaning back just far enough so that he could brush away the glint of tears away from her cheeks.

'Hey. Don't cry, gorgeous. I'm going to be right there with you, every step of the way.'

And he was kissing her again, pressing his soft lips against her throat and tilting his head so he could reach the sensitive skin on her neck.

Her eyes closed and she leant back just a little farther, arching her spine, supported by his long fingers as they slid down to her hips. Lexi stopped breathing and inwardly screamed in frustration because her body was enjoying itself far too much for her to reply. And her heart and mind sang.

She closed her eyes tight shut and focused on the sound of her own breathing. Only it was rather difficult when the man she wanted to be with was holding her so lovingly, keeping her steady on her wobbly legs, her toes clenched with tension inside her shoes.

Tempting her. Tempting her so badly she could taste it. She wanted him just as much as he wanted her. This was going to be their last night together, and…

No. If she gave in now there would be no going back. She would never be able to walk away. And neither would he. No matter how much she wanted to stay in his arms, she had to be brave for Mark's sake.

She just had to find the strength to get through this.

Lexi inhaled slowly, then whispered into Mark's shoulder, 'I don't think that would be a very good idea.' She dropped back so he would have to stop kissing her. 'In fact,' she continued in a trembling voice, 'it might be better if I started packing. I have an early flight tomorrow.'

The air escaped from his lungs in a slow, shuddering hot breath against her forehead.

It took her a few seconds to form the words she had to say. She was almost too afraid.

Her voice stayed calm, despite the thumping storm of confusion and resignation building in her chest. 'You know why we don't have a future together, Mark. You need to have a son to inherit your title and I can't give you one. And nothing we say or feel is going to change that fact.'

As soon as the words left her mouth she regretted them. The man who had been holding her so lovingly, unwilling to let her move out of his touch, stepped back. Moved away. Not physically, but emotionally.

The precious moment was gone. Trampled to fragments.

His face contorted with pain and closed down before her eyes. The warmth was gone, and she cursed herself for being so clumsy.

She had lost him.

'I was never supposed to be Baron Belmont,' Mark replied, his voice low and rough. 'That was my brother's job. Ed was the heir apparent, my parents' pride and joy. As far as my parents were concerned Edmund was the golden boy, the eldest son, whom they'd groomed since junior school to take over the company business and the estate. So when he died…it destroyed the family plans completely. And broke my mother's heart forever. It was as simple as that. The entire family collapsed.'

He looked into Lexi's face and smoothed back her hair with his fingertips.

'I was the second son, Lexi. As different from Edmund and my father as it was possible to be. I had to leave my world behind and take over the obligations that came with being the next Baron Belmont. I had no choice. I *had* to take over as the next heir. And everything that comes with it. Including making sure that I married early and produced a son to carry on the name.'

He closed his eyes. 'Working on my mother's biography has shown me just how much I've sacrificed to take his place—and how much I need to claw back my right to personal happiness. And that means *you,* Lexi.'

'You know that I can't have children.' Her voice quivered as she formed the syllables, and she only just managed the words before her voice failed. 'But you can. And that is why I have to let you go.'

Mark shook his head slowly and his chin dropped so their foreheads were touching. His breath was hot against her skin as the words came stumbling out. 'I can see where this is going, but you are *so* wrong. I want you and only you. Can you understand that?'

Lexi took a slow breath and squeezed her eyes tight shut, willing away the tears. 'And I want you. So very much. I'd given up hope of ever finding someone to love. But you need to have a son of your own. Somewhere out there is a very lucky woman you can cherish and who will be able to give you that son. And it's not me.'

'Another woman? Oh, Lexi.'

He straightened and drew back, physically holding her away from him. Her hands slid down his arms, desperate to hold on to the intensity of their connection, and her words babbled out in confusion and fear.

'We had a wonderful few days together, Mark. And I am so grateful to you for that.'

He'd turned away from her now, and paced back towards the bench, one hand clenched onto the back of his neck

'Grateful? Is that it? You're *grateful?* How can you walk away from what we have? I know you care about me, Lexi—please don't try and deny it.'

The bitterness in his voice was such a contrast to the loving man she'd just been holding that Lexi took a breath before answering. 'I do care about you—more than I can say. Can't you see? That's why the last thing I want to do is trap you into a relationship which will end in bitterness and disappointment, no matter how hard we both try.' She stepped forward and gently laid her hand on his arm as she looked into his face. 'You know I'm right. You're going to be a wonderful father, Mark. I just know it.'

She gulped away the burning sensation in her throat and looked into those wonderful eyes, so full of concern, and told him the truth—because nothing else would do.

'This is breaking my heart, Mark. I can't be with you any more. It's time to escape this perfect fantasy and get back to our ordinary lives. And if you love me then you have to let me go, Mark. Let me go. While we still have our precious love intact.'

'Lexi!'

The only thing that stopped Mark from running after her down the gravel footpath that led back to the villa was the heartbreak in her words and the unavoidable truth that he *did* love her—enough to stand, frozen, and watch her walk away.

Lexi sat in the very front row of the hydrofoil, facing the bow window at the front, so that her head was right in front of the TV showing cartoons with the sound off.

Her once-white linen trousers were a total mess, her blouse worse, and the only shoes she had with her were the flat tan leather sandals that Mark had bought her after they'd shared lunch that day in Gaios.

The elegant Greek woman sitting to her left was totally absorbed with cuddling and kissing a black toy poodle with red bows in its curls, which was getting ready to doze off for the hour-long journey.

Lexi was vaguely aware of tourists with their suitcases being loaded on at the harbour, filling up the seats behind her, their voices a blend of English and Italian accents. Some were yawning with the happy contentment of a sunny early morning call, but most were chatting away, couples and families enjoying the last day of their holiday before flying home.

She envied them that serenity. Her mind was a maelstrom of confused emotions and regret and loss, and she hadn't even left the island yet.

She felt as though time had stood still since she'd last spoken to Mark at the viewpoint.

It had taken only minutes to strip off her dress when she got back to the villa alone, to throw on the same trousers and loose blouse she'd been wearing that morning and cram everything from the wardrobe and drawers into her bags. He had not returned by the time her luggage was loaded into the car.

The cats had been sitting on the wall of sun-warmed stone as she'd turned the car around and driven through the wide entrance and onto the main road. When Snowy One had sat up and called to her she'd almost lost the will to go ahead with it.

Coward! She should have waited for him to come back. But that would have meant staying the night in the villa. And she was just not up to it. She would have given in and spent the night in his arms. And not regretted a second of it. That was the hard part.

Instead she'd held herself together long enough to drive down a country sideroad near Loggos and park her car well off the road, under the trees and away from the traffic and houses, before finally surrendering to the tears and anguish and exhaustion of the day. At some point in the night she'd fallen into an uncomfortable sleep for an hour or two before light broke through the trees above her.

She'd dropped her luggage off at the travel agent in Gaios when she'd handed back the hire car just as soon as the office opened that morning. She didn't need her expensive gowns and shoes for where she was going. This time her suitcases would be travelling cargo by themselves, and at this precise moment she really couldn't care less if they made it back to London or not. Everything she needed, everything she could not replace, was either in her huge shoulder bag or carried safe inside her heart. Where it would be locked away forever.

The burning in her throat emerged as a whispered sob, muffled by the sound of the hydrofoil engines starting up.

The sea was as smooth as a mirror, with only a gentle ripple to reflect back the jewelled sparkling of the rising sun. It was stunningly beautiful. A new hot sunny morning had dawned and her heart was breaking. She looked out of the hydrofoil windows, streaked with droplets of salt water from the seaspray.

The dew on the windows reflected back the fractured image of a woman who'd thought she knew what she wanted and had been proved completely wrong by someone so remarkable, so talented and so very lovable, that it took her breath away just thinking about him.

He would be awake now—if he had managed to sleep at all.

She wiped at the glass as the hydrofoil moved out into open water and headed towards Corfu, leaving behind the narrow green strip of the island with its white limestone cliffs that formed her last sight of Paxos. And the man she loved.

CHAPTER ELEVEN

MARK stood under the shade of the huge oak tree at the bottom of the drive as Cassie's golden retriever went tearing off across the lawn in search of a squirrel.

He looked up into the flame-tinged dark green and russet oak leaves above his head, so familiar to him that he sometimes forgot that tall oak trees from Belmont had been used to build the great wooden sailing ships that had made up the navy for so many kings and queens over the centuries.

Belmont's heritage. *His* heritage. And now he was paying the price for that.

Mark turned and started walking down the driveway between the two rows of mighty oak trees, back towards the magnificent Elizabethan manor house that was his family home. Belmont Manor.

The September late-afternoon sunshine had turned the buff old limestone to a warm, welcoming glow that brought to mind old hearths and the long history of the generations who had lived there. Purple and red ivy tinged with green clambered up the right block of the E-shaped house, but ended well below the curved stone decoration on each turret.

It was a solid house, almost six hundred years old, and barely changed over the centuries because the men had either been in London at court or busy fighting for their country. The heavy stone walls were broken up by rows of narrow mullioned windows which filled the rooms with coloured light, but never quite enough.

Looking at it now through fresh eyes, he couldn't fail to be impressed by the grandeur of the huge house. And yet this was his home. The place where he'd spent the first ten years of his life until he was sent to boarding school. But even then he'd come home to Belmont most weekends and every holiday. And he'd totally taken it for granted—just as he had with so much else in his life. Such as parents who would always be there to welcome him home, and a brother who would inherit the title and the house and all the obligations that went with it. Leaving the second son free to live his own life.

That was then. This was now.

Time to make a few changes.

Mark walked slowly through the beautiful timbered hallway and chuckled to himself at what Lexi would make of the suit of armour standing in the corner, and the family shields over the huge stone fireplace. She would probably want to wear the armour and invent some entirely inappropriate alternative descriptions for the heraldic symbols on the shields.

But as he strolled down the narrow oak-panelled corridor towards his father's study his smile faded. Everywhere he looked there was something to remind him of his mother. A Chinese flower vase or a stunning Tudor portrait, perfectly matched to the oak panelling and the period of the house. Right down to the stunning needlepoint panels which decorated the heavy oak doors. She'd always had the knack of finding the perfect item to decorate each room with such loving care and detail. It had taken her thirty years to do it, but in the process she'd transformed the dark and gloomy house he'd seen in family photographs into a warm, light family home.

This house was a celebration of her life, and Lexi had helped him to see that. Helped him to see a lot of things about his life in a new light.

He didn't need to be here in person today. He could have simply telephoned. But that was the coward's way out and he was through with that way of life. He had left that behind on Paxos three months ago.

Lifting his chin and squaring his shoulders, Mark strolled up to the half-open door and pushed it wide. His father looked up from his usual leather chair and waved at him to come closer. The gaunt look following his cancer treatment had faded. Charles Belmont was still slight, but he'd put on weight and was looking much more like the towering captain of industry and natural leader he had always been.

'Mark, my boy. Great to see you. Come and take a look at this. The advance copies of your mother's book arrived this morning. The printers have done a half-decent job.'

His father lifted up the hardback book and passed it to Mark, who had chosen to stand, rather than sit in the chair on the opposite side of the desk from his father as though he had come for a job interview.

'Excellent choice of photographs. Natural. I could not have chosen better myself. You did a remarkable job, Mark. Remarkable.'

And to Mark's horror Charles touched his nose with his knuckle to cover up his emotion. Strange: Mark did exactly the same thing and had never noticed it before.

Mark looked away and made a show of examining the cover's dust jacket and flicking through the first pages of his mother's biography. The publishers had chosen the very first photograph that Lexi had picked up that day on

Paxos, of his mother at the village fete. She looked happy and natural and full of life.

The photo worked brilliantly.

'Thank you, Father. But I can't take the credit for going with this particular photograph. That was Lexi's Sloane's idea. She thought it might help if people saw the real Crystal Leighton instead of some shallow movie star.'

'Damn right.' His father nodded. 'The girl's got a good head on her shoulders. And it did you good to meet someone outside the business world.' He nodded towards the book. 'I didn't just mean the cover. The stories you tell and your memories of happy and not-so-happy times brought her back to me in a way I didn't think possible. I don't have the talent for it. You clearly do.'

His voice dropped and he sat back in his chair, legs outstretched, tapping his fingers on the desk.

'Your sister is worried about you, Mark. When your mother was alive you would talk about what was happening in your life. But now…? I don't know what's going on in your head. We talk about the business—yes, sure. You even convinced me to go ahead with converting the cottages, and so far we're right on track with that risky business plan of yours. But since you got back from Greece you haven't been the same man. What do you want? More control of the business? The manor? Shout it out, son.'

'What do I want?'

Mark put down the book, strolled over to the window and looked out across the sunlit lawns. This was the first time in many, many years that his father had even asked him how he spent his day, but it was true that he had changed. They both had.

'Actually, I've been asking myself the same question an awful lot since I got back from Paxos. And the answers are not always comfortable,' he replied.

'Tough questions demand tough answers,' his father muttered dismissively. 'Let's hear it.'

Mark half turned back towards him. 'I want to stop feeling guilty for the fact that my mother couldn't tell me she didn't feel pretty enough to stand by me at my engagement party. That would be a start. I know now that there was nothing I could have done differently at the time,' he added softly, 'but it still makes me angry that she didn't trust us enough to share her pain.'

'Of course it makes you angry,' his father replied with a sniff. 'She didn't tell me, either. I thought she was perfect in every way. I can't understand her decision any more than you can. But she was an adult, intelligent woman who knew what she was doing. And don't you *dare* think it was about your blasted engagement. Because it wasn't. It was about her own self-worth. And if you're angry—fine. We can be angry together.'

The tapping continued.

'What else is on that list of yours? What about this girl who helped write the book?'

Mark took a moment to stay calm before making his reply. 'Actually, she's the reason I'm here today. Lexi has it in her head that marrying a girl who can give me a son is more important to me than finding someone I want to spend the rest of my life with. Three months ago she might have been right. Not any more. Not now.' He looked over his shoulder and made eye contact. 'I'm sorry, Father, but chances are that Lexi and I will *not* be able to give you the grandson you were hoping for. The Belmont line will probably end with me.'

The air between Mark and his father almost crackled with the fierce electricity of the tension between them.

'Even if it means that the title passes to your cousin Rupert? The spoiled brat who threw you out of a boat on the lake when you wouldn't let him row? This girl must mean a great deal to you.'

'She does. More than I can say.'

Mark heard the creak of the leather chair behind him, but didn't turn around to his father because of the tears in his eyes. A strong, warm arm wrapped around his shoulders and hugged him just once, then dropped to the window frame so they were both looking out in the same direction.

The intimate contact was slight, but so incredibly new that it seemed to break down the final barrier Mark had been holding between himself and his father for so many years. They had made real progress over these past three months, but this was new. He turned his head towards him.

'I'm pleased to hear that you've met someone at long last. I had almost given up on you. From what Cassie tells me, Alexis is not responsible for what her father did. She loves you enough to do the right thing, and sacrificed her personal happiness for yours. In my book that makes her someone I would like to meet. You deserve to have some love in your life, Mark. Your mother was right. You should get out more.'

He nodded once, then gestured with his head towards the book on his desk.

'If there's one thing your mother's story tells us it's that we loved her and she loved us. More than we knew. And in the end that's the only thing that matters. I am jolly glad that Crystal Leighton came into my life and made me the happiest man alive for so many wonderful years. And gave me my three wonderful children. I blame myself for what happened after Edmund. Tough times. Hard to deal with. I was not up to the job.'

Then he looked up into the sky and his voice turned wistful. 'I should be the one apologising to you, not the other way round. You're right. Don't give your inheritance another thought. The future can take care of itself. You're the man I always knew you could be, and I'm proud to have you as my son.'

Mark took a deep breath and startled his father by giving him a slap on the back. 'I'm pleased to hear it—because I'm heading off to London tomorrow to try and persuade her to give me another chance. Thanks, Dad. I'm pleased you like the book. And thank you even more for bringing Lexi Sloane into my life.'

'What are you waiting here for? Go get your girl and bring her home so she can meet the family. And don't you frighten her off with all this pressure about having sons. It's about time we had some fun around here.'

Dratted device. Lexi shook the small battery-powered sander in the vain hope that playing maracas with it would actually squeeze out enough power to finish the living-room wall.

No such luck. The sander gave a low whine and then shuddered to a halt as the battery gave out.

'Oh, come on, you stupid thing,' she snapped. 'I charged you for three hours this morning. The least you could do is work.'

She sat down on the arm of the sofa in the middle of the room. It was covered with a dust sheet and had been for weeks, while she stripped off the old wallpaper and repaired the holes in the plaster. Now came the dusty part. Sanding away the bumpy walls until they were smooth.

For the last twelve weeks Lexi had filled her days and nights with work that should have provided the perfect distraction.

But it was no use.

Apparently no amount of physical hard work on the

house could replace her obsession for Mark Belmont. He filled her days and nights with dreams and fantasies of what could have been; what had been lost. Worse, every time she looked at her children's stories of kittens having great adventures she was transported back in her mind's eye to the original inspiration and the sunny garden of Mark's villa on Paxos. The wonderful house and the man who owned it.

She could only hope that he wasn't as miserable as she was. Even if the view was particularly delightful from the balcony of his no doubt sumptuous penthouse apartment.

With a low sigh, Lexi replaced the sander on its charger and turned off the trance music that was giving her a headache.

She needed air.

Lexi walked the few steps from the living room to her freshly decorated kitchen, grabbed some juice out of the refrigerator and stepped out onto the tiny patio where she had replaced the traditional redbrick paving with buff-coloured sandstone slabs. Bright red geraniums and herbs spilled out from terracotta pots close to the kitchen door, and a simple wooden trellis still carried the last of the climbing roses.

A precious ray of September sunshine warmed her face and the tiny olive bush in the brightly coloured pot she had painted next to her wooden chair. The colour on the paint tin had been described as 'Mediterranean Blue.' But it was not the same. How could it be? Nothing in her life could be the same again.

She was still standing in the sunshine watching the sparrows on the bird table ten minutes later, when the front doorbell rang. She jogged back to fling it open, a pencil still logged behind one ear, expecting to see the postman.

It was not the postman.

'Mark?' she gasped, staring at him, hardly able to believe her eyes. 'What are you doing here? I thought you'd moved to—'

'No. I changed my mind about New York. I'm having way too much fun right here in Blighty.'

She swallowed and then gave a low sigh, blinking away tears.

He was here. On her doorstep. Tall, gorgeous and overwhelmingly tinglicious.

'Is your dad okay? I saw the pictures from the film festival when he accepted that lifetime achievement award on behalf of your mum. He looked a bit shaky.'

He reached out and touched her arm, his fingers light on the sleeve of her boiler suit. 'Dad's fine. He's still recovering, but he'll stick around long enough to make my life interesting for some time to come. Thanks for asking. The emotion of the night got to all of us. I'm sorry you weren't there to help us celebrate.'

There was an awkward pause, and just when her resolve gave way and she felt that she simply had to say something, *anything,* to fill the silence, Mark suddenly presented her with a gift-wrapped square package tied with a silver ribbon.

'I know that you'd prefer me not to contact you, but I thought you might want to have your personal copy of the biography. Signed, of course,' he said, his voice dry and hesitant. 'My dad is planning a private launch party in a few weeks, so this is a sneak peek. And, by the way, the Belmont family would love to have you there. It wouldn't be the same if I couldn't thank you in person on the big night. I haven't forgotten what you said. You deserve the credit for making this book a reality.'

She looked at the package, then back to Mark in silence, and then her shoulders dropped about six inches and she slid the yellow washing-up glove from one hand and wrapped her fingers around the book. She pulled it towards her for a second, then looked down at the paint splattered overalls and socks she was wearing and shrugged.

'Sanding. Plastering. Bit of a mess. Not sure I'm ready for smart book-launch parties.'

'You look lovely,' he replied in a totally serious voice, but his eyes and mouth were smiling as his gaze locked onto hers. 'You look like *you.*'

He tilted his head to one side and gave her a lopsided grin which made him look about twelve years old.

And her poor lonely heart melted all over again.

'What have you been doing with yourself these past few months?' he whispered. 'Travelling the world? Seeing the sights? Tell me about all the wonderful exotic locations your clients have whisked you away to. Africa? Asia?'

She smiled back, her defences weakened by the wonderful charm and warmth of this man who was standing so very close and yet seemed beyond reach.

'Actually, I've been working on my own projects right here.' She waved her right hand in the air and looked up at the ornate plasterwork ceiling of her hallway. 'I thought that I might stay in one place for a while.' Her voice quivered a little and the silver bow on the gift-wrapping suddenly became the focus of her attention. 'Try and get my bearings after...'

She swallowed, almost losing control at the thought of Paxos, and quickly changed the subject. 'But I can see what *you've* been doing,' she whispered, giving him a half smile. 'You finished the book. Does you dad love it as much as you hoped?'

'He does. He had to go back into hospital for another round of chemotherapy. It was tough. But when I brought the manuscript in to check on a few details... It was one of the few times in my life that my father has held my hand and cried. Going through the chapters together changed us. Made us talk about things I had put off for way too long. It was good. Actually, it was better than good. It was grand. What was the phrase you used? Oh, yes. *Awesome sauce.* The book is awesome sauce. And I have you to thank for making that happen.'

'Not just me. He should be proud of you.' Lexi stroked the wrapping and pressed her lips together, her mind reeling from the fact that Mark was so close. She longed to touch and hold him and tell him how much she had desperately missed him... But she knew that would only make things a lot worse.

'I'll read it later, if you don't mind. I need to get back to my decorating.' She waved her yellow glove back inside the hallway. 'Lots to do.' She half turned to step back inside, then glanced back at him over her shoulder. 'But thank you for bringing me this in person. I hope it gets stunning reviews and puts some ghosts to bed. For all of us. Good luck, Mark. To you and your family.'

Time stood still for a few seconds as Lexi remained in the doorway, hating to say goodbye.

'Lexi. Can I come in? Just for five minutes? I really do need to talk to you.' Then he pulled back his arm and shook his head. 'Forget that. That's what the old Mark would have said.'

He stepped forward so quickly that Lexi was still taking in a sharp breath when he wrapped his arms around her back and pulled her sharply towards him. Looking into her startled eyes, Mark smiled and pulled her even tighter, so that the only thing separating their bodies was the book he had just given her.

'I would much rather have this conversation on your doorstep, so that the whole of London can hear me tell you that I've been totally miserable these past few months without my sparkly Lexi by my side. In fact I missed your irritating sparkliness so much that I stopped being grumpy and decided to be a better man, instead.'

Her heart turned a somersault. 'Oh, you were grumpy. But I wasn't always sparkly, so I think we're about even.'

'Sparkly enough for me. And please don't make me lose my place in my speech. I was just getting to the apology—where I grovel at your feet and beg your forgiveness for being such an idiot that I let you go without fighting harder to persuade you to stay.'

'In that case I shall try not to be sparkly. Because I quite like the sound of that part.'

'I rather thought you might. Only I'm a bit out of practice when it comes to grovelling. In fact, this is a first, so you'll have to forgive me if I get it wrong.'

Lexi tugged off her other glove and pressed her free hand onto Mark's chest. He inhaled deeply with pleasure at her touch.

'On the contrary.' She smiled. 'I think you grovel quite beautifully. But you can stop now. There's something I'd like to show you.'

She grabbed his hand and half dragged him down the narrow hall and into the kitchen of her tiny terraced house.

'Do you remember all the photographs I took of your kittens on the terrace at the villa? Well, here they are.'

She pointed to the row of printed pages which ran the full length of the kitchen wall. 'On the left side of the page is a photo of the kittens, and then on the right side are a few lines of the story.'

'Is that Snowy One peeping his head out from my stone wall?' Mark asked, laughing at the cutest white kitten with pink ears, pinker tongue and a cheeky grin. 'It is—and here's Snowy Two, halfway up the trunk of the olive tree next to the table-tennis table. I think it was the moment when it dawned on him that going down might be slightly trickier than climbing up. "Once upon a time in the land of sunshine there lived a family of positively pampered cats,'" Mark read slowly, then snorted and looked back at Lexi. 'Well, that certainly is true. My housekeeper feeds them chicken when I'm away!'

Lexi took a step to his side and read out the rest of the page. "'There was a mummy cat, a daddy cat and two kittens. Their real names were Snowy and Smudge, but most days they ended up being called other names—like rascal, scamp, trouble and mischief.'"

'Oh, that is perfect. These are wonderful, Lexi.' He sighed warmly and walked, with her hand still held in his, from photograph to photograph. 'I knew you were talented. But these are magical. Truly wonderful. Cassie's boys would adore these stories.'

Lexi paused and looked up into his face. 'But not *my* boys, Mark. I know there's a small chance that medically I could have your son, but lurching from month to month with hope and then disappointment is no way to live. It wouldn't be fair on either of us. And that hasn't gone away.'

'No, it hasn't,' he replied, lifting a strand of hair and pushing it back over her forehead as he slid away her bandanna. 'But I know now that a life without love in it is no life at all. *You* are the only woman I want in my life. Plus I'm going to need some help with childcare. Ah…yes.' He smiled at her stunned face. 'That reminds me. I should probably mention that I plan to adopt. Two girls and two boys would work well, but I'm flexible. There are an awful lot of children out there who need a loving home where they can be spoiled rotten, and I suspect that we would be very good at that.'

'Adopt? Four children? You would do that for me?' Lexi

asked, suddenly feeling faint, horrified, stunned, amazed and thrilled to the core.

'In a heartbeat.' Mark shrugged and drew her closer. 'You are the girl for me. And that's it. Those children will be blessed with the most wonderful mum. And I'm going to be right there every step of the way. In fact, I'm rather looking forward to being a dad.'

'Wait a minute,' Lexi replied and shook her head. 'You seem to be forgetting something very important here. I was the one who couldn't face the hard time ahead of us. Not you. I was the coward. You made me feel loved and treasured, and it was so intense and so beautiful I couldn't deal with it, Mark. I just couldn't believe it was possible that any man could love me so much. And I ran. And I shouldn't have. I should have stayed and fought harder to make it work. I am sorry for that. I just couldn't believe it was real. I couldn't believe you wanted me.'

Her head lolled forward so that her dirty, dusty forehead was resting on his beautiful dark suit.

'Believe it,' he murmured, his chin pressed on top of her hair. 'Because it's true.'

He tipped her chin up so that she could look into his eyes, and the intensity and depth of what she saw there choked her so much that her breath came out in deep sobs.

'I telephoned your mother yesterday and personally invited her to the book launch. She was a tad surprised to hear from me, but we got along splendidly after I mentioned that I am completely besotted with her daughter and my sole objective in life from this moment is her complete happiness.'

'You said that to my mum?' Lexi gasped. 'Wow. That must have been an interesting conversation. You do know that she'll hold you to it? Wait a minute… I spoke to her last night and she never said a word.'

'Um… We made a pact. She wouldn't tell you that I was coming round so long as I promised to kidnap you from your world of plastering and whisk you off to a luxury hotel for an afternoon of pampering in the spa, a fine meal and hopefully some debauchery.'

She slumped against him. 'Oh, that sounds so good.'

'There's more. Your delightful and charming parent happened to mention that your home-decorating project was sucking time away from your writing. This cannot be permitted to continue. Children everywhere need to see these stories as soon as possible.'

He grinned and winked. 'The Belmont estate has a wonderful team of builders and decorators who will be happy to help my girlfriend in her hour of need. They are currently on standby, ready to burst into action at a moment's notice and get busy on your charming London house while you spend the weekend with my family at the manor.'

'That's—that's very generous, but I couldn't possibly accept… And…girlfriend? What manor? And you winked at me. You *winked*. Things really have changed.'

'I thought it was about time I started to be spontaneous. And I was hoping that if I played my cards right you might let me share this bijou gem of a home with you. It's far better than any clinical, empty penthouse. And, best of all, you are in it.'

He cupped Lexi's head between his hands, his long fingers so gentle and tender and loving that her heart melted even more.

'I love you, Alexis Sloane. I love everything about you. I love that you are a survivor. I love that you have come through so much and still have so much love to give to the world. I am so proud of everything you have achieved, and I want to be there when you go on to even greater things. I believe in your talent and I want to share my life with you.'

'You love me?'

He nodded. 'Yep. I love you. All of you. Especially that part of you that doesn't believe that she deserves to be loved. Because that's the bit I fit into. Say yes, Lexi. Say *yes*. Take the risk and let me into your life. Because you are not a coward. Far from it. You are the bravest woman I have ever met.'

'I would have to be brave to be *your* girlfriend,' she sobbed, spreading tears and plaster dust all over his suit. 'But give me ten minutes to get packed and I'll show you how much I've missed you every second of every day we have been apart.'

'You don't need to pack. Where we're going clothing is entirely optional.'

'Oh, I *do* love you,' she replied, flinging her arms around his neck and kissing him with every ounce of devotion and passion and repressed longing that she could collect into one kiss—a kiss that had them both panting when she released him.

'Wow.' He grinned, blinking, gasping for breath, his eyes locked on hers. 'Really?'

'*Really,* really. I love you so very, very much. Enough to stand up to anyone who even tries to break us apart. No matter who it is. Oh, Mark, I've missed you so much.'

His hands stroked her face and he grinned, his eyes sparkling with energy and life. 'Excellent. Because I've already invited your mother and her fiancé to meet the Belmont clan at the manor tomorrow. I cannot wait a moment longer to show you off.'

She gasped. 'My mother? And Baron Belmont? Now, *that's* something I want to see. He won't know what's hit him.'

'I have no doubt. But they're all going to have to get used to the idea. This is the first day of the rest of our lives,

Lexi. Tell me what you want to do and where you want to go and I'll take you there.'

Lexi took in a long breath and looked into the face of the man she loved—the man who loved her in return and was offering her the world on a golden platter. 'Then take me back to Paxos and that secret garden on a clifftop. And this time we are going to watch the sunset together. Forever.'

EPILOGUE

LEXI strolled into the luxurious reception room of one of London's most exclusive gentlemen's clubs and paused to take in the sumptuous interior which had already sent her mother into raptures over the ornate plasterwork, stunning Art Nouveau statuary and hand-painted Chinese wallpaper.

Deep brocade-covered sofas and crystal chandeliers added to the opulence—but they were lost on Lexi. Her high-heeled sandals sank into the fine Oriental carpet as she stood on tiptoe to find the one person she needed and wanted so badly to be with on his special day.

And there he was. Elegant in his favourite charcoal cashmere suit and the pale pink shirt she had ironed for him that afternoon, chatting away to Cassie and his mother's showbiz friends in front of a huge white marble fireplace. His father had one arm around Mark's shoulder and was laughing out loud, his head back, relaxed and happy, as one of London's most famous theatre actors shared an anecdote about the old days when he worked with Crystal.

The love and the warmth of the scene added to the familiar heat that flashed through her body the moment she saw Mark's eyes focus on her from across the room, inviting her to join him.

Clusters of elegant people were gathered around the tables, flicking through the pages of *Mrs Belmont's Lemon Cake,* some smiling and some wiping away tears. All affected by the woman Mark had captured so brilliantly in the pages of a book that was surely going to soar up the best-seller lists.

Her reward for wending her way across the room was a warm hug from Cassie and a kiss on the cheek from Charles. But it was Mark who gathered her to him, his arm wrapped tightly around the waist of her simple pleated silk plum cocktail dress so that she was locked into his side.

'You look even more amazing than normal, Miss Sloane. And that is saying something!' he whispered into her hair.

'Well, thank you, Mr Belmont, but I think the jewellery might have something to do with that.' She grinned, pressing one hand to his mother's stunning diamond-and-sapphire necklace which Mark had placed around her neck only minutes before they'd been due to leave her house for the party.

'Oh, no. You are already sparkly enough for me. This is just a finishing touch for the rest of the world to see.'

The sides of his mouth lifted into an intimate smile that made her heart soar as he tapped the end of her nose.

'Ah. Lexi. There you are.' The smiling owner of Brightmore Press charged forward, waving the biography in his hand. 'Splendid job. Just splendid. Huge success. I need to say a few words to our guests, but I'll be right back.' He looked at her over the top of his black spectacles. 'And don't you *dare* leave before we have a chat about that series of children's books you've promised me. I've already booked a page in our Christmas catalogue. Catch you later!'

He sped off to grab Baron Belmont.

Mark squeezed Lexi's waist as she smiled up into his

face. 'Well, I suppose I shall have to get used to having my own name on the cover for a change.'

'This is only the start,' Mark replied, then laughed out loud. 'They already know that I couldn't have written this book without you. Get ready for the time of your life, Miss Awesome Sauce. There's no holding you back now—and I am going to be right there by your side, cheering you on. All the way.'

* * * * *

Mills & Boon® Hardback

June 2012

ROMANCE

A Secret Disgrace	Penny Jordan
The Dark Side of Desire	Julia James
The Forbidden Ferrara	Sarah Morgan
The Truth Behind his Touch	Cathy Williams
Enemies at the Altar	Melanie Milburne
A World She Doesn't Belong To	Natasha Tate
In Defiance of Duty	Caitlin Crews
In the Italian's Sights	Helen Brooks
Dare She Kiss & Tell?	Aimee Carson
Waking Up In The Wrong Bed	Natalie Anderson
Plain Jane in the Spotlight	Lucy Gordon
Battle for the Soldier's Heart	Cara Colter
It Started with a Crush...	Melissa McClone
The Navy Seal's Bride	Soraya Lane
My Greek Island Fling	Nina Harrington
A Girl Less Ordinary	Leah Ashton
Sydney Harbour Hospital: Bella's Wishlist	Emily Forbes
Celebrity in Braxton Falls	Judy Campbell

HISTORICAL

The Duchess Hunt	Elizabeth Beacon
Marriage of Mercy	Carla Kelly
Chained to the Barbarian	Carol Townend
My Fair Concubine	Jeannie Lin

MEDICAL

Doctor's Mile-High Fling	Tina Beckett
Hers For One Night Only?	Carol Marinelli
Unlocking the Surgeon's Heart	Jessica Matthews
Marriage Miracle in Swallowbrook	Abigail Gordon

0512 GEN STD HB

ROMANCE

An Offer She Can't Refuse	Emma Darcy
An Indecent Proposition	Carol Marinelli
A Night of Living Dangerously	Jennie Lucas
A Devilishly Dark Deal	Maggie Cox
The Cop, the Puppy and Me	Cara Colter
Back in the Soldier's Arms	Soraya Lane
Miss Prim and the Billionaire	Lucy Gordon
Dancing with Danger	Fiona Harper

HISTORICAL

The Disappearing Duchess	Anne Herries
Improper Miss Darling	Gail Whitiker
Beauty and the Scarred Hero	Emily May
Butterfly Swords	Jeannie Lin

MEDICAL

New Doc in Town	Meredith Webber
Orphan Under the Christmas Tree	Meredith Webber
The Night Before Christmas	Alison Roberts
Once a Good Girl...	Wendy S. Marcus
Surgeon in a Wedding Dress	Sue MacKay
The Boy Who Made Them Love Again	Scarlet Wilson

Mills & Boon® Hardback

July 2012

ROMANCE

MEDICAL

612 GEN STD HB

Mills & Boon® Large Print

July 2012

ROMANCE

Roccanti's Marriage Revenge	Lynne Graham
The Devil and Miss Jones	Kate Walker
Sheikh Without a Heart	Sandra Marton
Savas's Wildcat	Anne McAllister
A Bride for the Island Prince	Rebecca Winters
The Nanny and the Boss's Twins	Barbara McMahon
Once a Cowboy...	Patricia Thayer
When Chocolate Is Not Enough...	Nina Harrington

HISTORICAL

The Mysterious Lord Marlowe	Anne Herries
Marrying the Royal Marine	Carla Kelly
A Most Unladylike Adventure	Elizabeth Beacon
Seduced by Her Highland Warrior	Michelle Willingham

MEDICAL

The Boss She Can't Resist	Lucy Clark
Heart Surgeon, Hero...Husband?	Susan Carlisle
Dr Langley: Protector or Playboy?	Joanna Neil
Daredevil and Dr Kate	Leah Martyn
Spring Proposal in Swallowbrook	Abigail Gordon
Doctor's Guide to Dating in the Jungle	Tina Beckett

0612 GEN STD LP